Kiss Me

Merry Christmas
Grant and Allyson
from Paul

Xmas 96

Kiss Me

Andrew Pyper

The Porcupine's Quill

CANADIAN CATALOGUING IN PUBLICATION DATA

Pyper, Andrew, 1968-
 Kiss me

ISBN 0-88984-181-0

I. Title.

PS8581.Y64K5 1996   C813'.54   C96-931156-7
PR9199.3.P96K5 1996

Published by The Porcupine's Quill, Inc., 68 Main Street, Erin, Ontario NOB 1TO, with financial assistance from The Canada Council and the Ontario Arts Council. The support of the Department of Canadian Heritage through the Book and Periodical Industry Development programme and the Periodical Distribution Assistance Programme is also gratefully acknowledged.

This is a work of fiction. Any resemblance of characters to persons, living or dead, is purely co-incidental.

Represented in Canada by the Literary Press Group. Trade orders are available from General Distribution Services.

Readied for the press by John Metcalf. Copy edited by Doris Cowan. Cover art is after a photograph by Alex Beckett.

Typeset in Ehrhardt, printed on Zephyr Antique Laid, sewn into signatures and bound at The Porcupine's Quill.

Contents

Acknowledgements

The following must be thanked for their help to me and/or the book:

The journals in which many of these stories or versions of these stories originally appeared, namely *The New Quarterly, Event, Quarry, Descant, Blood & Aphorisms,* and *The Quarterly;*

The Ontario Arts Council, for financial support;

Stephen Heighton, for his kindness and advice;

Leah Ross, for love, and for helping the characters act and speak the way they were supposed to;

All those who provided comments and criticism at the journals I submitted my work to, whether they accepted it or not, especially Mary Merikle, Kim Jernigan and Peter Hinchcliffe at *The New Quarterly* and Stephen Heighton and Mary Cameron at *Quarry;*

All at The Porcupine's Quill, for their professionalism;

Alex Beckett, for his striking and sometimes even flattering photography;

Diane Schoemperlen, Barbara Gowdy and Oakland Ross for their encouragements along the way;

and to John Metcalf, for his precise editing, honest opinions and his skill for making all the blurry images a little sharper.

For my Mother and my Father

Dime Bag Girl

SHE TRANSFERRED from Toronto at the beginning of term but was still considered new at school. This gave other kids an excuse to keep their distance, which they did anyway for other reasons. They were curious though, and told stories: why did she spend lunch sitting beside the single poplar tree in the endzone smoking American cigarettes and reading novels you didn't have to read for English? How could her father let her wear those state trooper shades to school? Everybody knew she was the one, or one of the ones, with the dope. Funny thing about that: her dad was circuit county judge. She had her own car, too. A Plymouth Duster. It had a front bench seat pock-burned by hash embers and a radio that for some reason only picked up AM country and western. That's all they knew. Surface and skin and habit. All the things that allowed them to keep her strange, a stranger, they knew all that. And that the two of us were each other's only friends. They knew that, too.

Now, what more would you like to know?

* * *

We lived in a small town on Lake Huron with an almost abandoned harbour, in which sat one or two rusty freighters waiting to take salt away from what was left in the tunnels dug under the beach, K-Mart, the Legion Hall, the lake itself. There was the high school we went to with cut-out snowflakes and Halloween witches on broomsticks all year round in the windows. A hotel occupied by drunks, two strippers rotating between the three taverns in the county that would have them, and a picture of the Queen over the bar. A street with elms where the rich lived. A red brick train station with the shingles rotting off and weeds growing high around the rails.

There wasn't much to do so we smoked drugs when we could get them. She bought them from a man called Buzzard who lived above Smythe's Shoe Store. Sometimes she'd take me with her, and we would sit on ratty easy chairs thick with grey dog hair, which was funny because Buzzard didn't own a dog. From these chairs we'd watch him fumble with his scales and divide the weed into neat piles with an X-Acto blade as though it were coke.

'How'd you get so pretty?' he asks her.

'C'mon, Buzz. Cut the shit. Let's go, man.'

'Hey, OK, pretty thing.'

Before handing it over he acts a little hurt, as if accusing us of only liking him for his drugs, which is true, in a way. It's just that it's the only thing that makes Buzzard interesting, that saves him from being an ugly, lonely man. And it doesn't entirely save him from this, anyway.

'Fly away, fly away,' he shoos us with a feigned bitterness. He has papery skin and a fat face and when he sulks he looks like a dried apple with stuck-in cloves for eyes. 'Have a *good* time,' he whispers at her. 'But you always do, right, beautiful?'

She gets up, the dime bag still hanging from her fingers and the green bud within it, captured and suspended in air like some rare insect. Then without a look we're moving, creaking down the muddy linoleum stairs, swiping dog hairs from our sweaters and jeans.

'My man, let's go to the beach,' she says, swinging open the driver's side door of the Duster. We don't put money in the meter because we never get tickets. The police have instructions from her dad.

'Brave new world,' I say, which is the thing I've decided to say these days.

I hit the radio and hold my eyes open wide until my forehead starts to get tired. I think: *This car is the best place I have known.* Steel guitar, eighteen inches of warm space between us, and ground into the vinyl seats and gummy carpet the spruce-needle smell of dope.

'Ah *yes*. A-*lone*, fi-nally,' she says in an accent she calls her Marlene Dietrich, and I laugh, not knowing who Marlene Dietrich is.

* * *

I never ask any questions about where her mother is or the

tender-looking pouches under her eyes, or the way she refers to her dad only by way of pronoun, as 'He' or 'Him'. She might have told me what the story was, but I was too much in love with her to know what to do if she did. I'm embarrassed now by the sound of those words – 'in love' – but how else do I say it without getting it wrong?

Her dad's navy blue Lincoln sat either in his gravel driveway or in his named spot outside the front doors of the courthouse, and those are the only places I ever saw him, getting in or climbing out of the dark leather cabin with deliberate shifts of bearish shoulders and broad ass. I never said a word to him. I never heard him speak.

There were rumours about her father which were fuelled by the absence of a wife, his non-attendance at any church, his disinclination to be a visible town leader. People would drive by his dark house just to take a look in the windows, which never told anyone anything. For these absent reasons nobody was surprised when, after they'd gone, the *Herald* carried a corner page blurb announcing that he had taken an extended leave from the bench and left the county to receive treatment for 'exhaustion.' After that there was a short while when people spoke of him and his strange daughter in regretful but satisfied tones, and then they stopped speaking of them at all.

But I don't know about any of that yet, driving down Ontario Street in the Duster that summer, two weeks shy of the end of school. I don't know anything when I ask why we never go over to her place, why I've never met the old man.

'Why would he give a fuck about you?' she says.

'We're friends. You and me, I mean.'

'He doesn't care about that. *Friends.* All his friends stopped calling a long time ago.'

'Why?'

'Because he married my mother and they had me. And what does that mean? That I just happen to be tied up in his fucked-up life and there's nothing I can do about it .'

'Don't say …'

'People owe people things. That's all.'

She could always bring an end to talking.

As we drive out of town I watch the harbour salt silos

shrink in the rear view mirror, wait for the blinking light of the water tower, the orange streetlights and revolving Dairy Queen sign to melt into a single, sad glow beside the black body of the lake. Out there, the water's so dark it eats the stars. That's what she said once.

Beside me she drives with one hand at the bottom of the wheel, the other moves around and runs through her hair, opens the window, fiddles with the radio. When she looks over at me it is with a warming, co-conspirator's grin. I think: *Every time with her is like goodbye.* A thrilled idea of never coming back.

'Roll one,' she says, passing me her silver cigarette case with her father's initials etched into it. Inside there is a lighter, Export papers, a sticky-tar safety pin and the leftover shake from Buzzard's last shipment wrapped in foil from a Coffee Crisp. I break our new bud apart over a *Barrister's Monthly* on my lap and get to work, looking out the window while my fingers crumble, gather and roll. From the highway you could look into the golden rooms of farmhouses and see motionless heads sitting on TV sofas, dogs chasing rabbits in the yard, blank-faced women in tank tops smoking on front porches.

'Wouldn't it be good to live on a farm?' I ask. 'You and me?'

'I wouldn't want to kill animals.'

'No animals. We'd plant seeds. Corn. We would walk through the corn and get lost in our own fields. Acres and acres.'

'Just roll.'

We get high and drive to the Conservation Area, park the car and smoke some more, maybe play the radio. Conway Twitty, Merle Haggard, Charley Pride, Hank Williams, and always Patsy Cline. If we feel like it, we go down to the beach and lie in the dunes, listen to the big lake come in easy on the sand. This is what we do almost every night when the weather's okay, just me and her. I can't dream of anything else.

'One of these days I'm going to just keep going. Drive right out of here,' she says, the car parked, her big-knuckled hands still on the wheel.

'Where would you go?'

'It wouldn't matter.'

Her eyes take me in and show something powerless and resigned, like shame.

'I'd go with you,' I say. 'It wouldn't matter to me, either.'

Then she kisses me. Her face comes in and her eyelids, blue from smoke, slowly shut. It's not passionate, that's not what it's about. But it is forgiving, grateful, and honest, like letting someone look at a scar.

'Thank God for you,' she says, pushing the hair back from my face. Her breath tastes of green basil and cherries. 'You're not like him at all. Not like any of them. Not at all.'

She says this as though it is a conclusion that has surprised her but not changed anything in her opinion of the larger world.

* * *

When she reaches the water she stops and undresses, leaving her clothes in a pile on the egg-shaped stones. Her body is lean and white in the darkness, her limbs fine and precise, an extraterrestrial. Then she starts in, laughing when a wave bumps into her, her body now a yellow flash of movement in the dark tide.

'It's so *cold!*' she shouts, and disappears beneath the surface. For a couple of seconds she's gone, and I think how easy it would be for her to never come back, to resurface on the rocks of Lake Superior and knock on the door of a hermit's shack to ask for a blanket and directions to the nearest lumber road. But then her head comes up again and her hands stroke her long hair against her head and she gives me a little wave to join her. Head cocked to one side, arm raised and bent at the elbow, her hand flat and circling. It would be impossible to ignore this wordless signal, although hardly detectable in the starless night. I feel her without seeing her, registering her body by a change in temperature, an invisible vibration of the air.

* * *

When we dry off and can't smoke any more, we climb into the Duster and creep back into town, the tires whispering past the dark windows of closed laundromats, the beer store, naked and dismembered mannequins gaping in a fabric shop. We don't talk much. Coming down for us is always a time of disembodied silence, not quite peaceful but something like that. We go back to her house, where she parks under the broad limbs of an old maple tree. 'I'm tired,' she says, and with her words I realize that I am as well. The weed and the cold lake water have made my body heavy and thick. The fifteen-minute walk to my house seems like a desert crossing.

'I'm just gonna sit here for a while,' I say, slouching down in the seat.

'Whatever. Just don't let my dad find you here in the morning. He'll have you arrested or something.'

She gets out and I watch her go in the side door of the house. My eyes linger on the path she's followed until they close. I sleep dreamlessly for what feels like a few hours until awakened by the muffled but persistent sounds of shouting, an argument. But it is only one voice. The judge, his voice vibrating outside the walls and windows of the house and into the leaf-breeze night outside. For a while I just sit and listen to it, strain to hear the words, to see the person who could make those sounds. The voice conveys anger but frailty also, something cut wide open.

After a while I get out of the car and crouch closer to the house. I linger beside the judge's professionally pruned rose bushes, listening to the voice trembling out of the curtained front window. I can see him only as a backlit shadow through the closed French doors at the far end of the dining room. He has stopped shouting and speaks in a held-back tone, standing still with his hands placed against the doors. I watch him across the dining-room table made of dark, expensive-looking wood. At one end is a ceramic ashtray painted in sickly yellows arched with cigarette butts, their orange heads huddled together in dunes of grey dust. The other end is blocked off by a fortress of serious magazines and *Globe and Mail*s. Behind the table is a glass cabinet full of Canadian Club and Gibson's, and on the wall paintings of ships crossing rough seas.

His voice is down to a normal level now, lower than normal, and it's impossible to tell what he's saying in complete sentences, but some of the words travel better than others. I hear 'never', 'bitch', 'tired', and 'mine'. Then the light goes out with him still standing there and there's nothing.

I want to go home but my feet sink further into the flower bed's soil. Then the sound of the back screen door closing with a careful latch. She comes from around the corner with her shoulders and head lowered in a half-attempt at hiding. She doesn't seem surprised when she sees me standing there in the middle of the front bushes.

'Nobody likes their father,' I say.

'It's not about *liking.*'

In the pale streetlight it looks like she is crying, but her voice is even and she had eyes that looked that way all the time anyway, so it was impossible to tell. Besides, she would hate me if I said something stupid like 'Don't cry' when she wasn't. So instead I lower my head along with hers and wait.

'Let's go for a drive,' she says finally, going into her suede purse for the keys.

'What? It's late.'

'Brave new world.'

'Shit, man, I gotta go home. I fell asleep …'

'I need to go for a drive. I need you to come with me.'

Need was all she had to say.

* * *

We park in the back corner of the Pizza Dee-Lite parking lot, a favourite spot because it's dark and overlooks the lake. We don't have any more dope so we just sit there for a long time without saying or doing anything. I knew I couldn't ask questions, she talked when she wanted to. And when she did it was to say, 'We're leaving the day after tomorrow.'

'Leaving? For how long?'

'Forever. We're moving. He thinks we're not far enough away yet.'

Now she really is crying, but softly, her shoulders still. Her voice is thin and the tears fall off her chin in steady drips. I want to hold her but I'm not sure I can.

'You don't know what it's like to know someone would die if it weren't for you. You don't.'

I want to say yes, I do, but it wouldn't be true.

She turns to me, and her eyes look directly into mine.

There is a softness in her face I've never seen before, an unguarded setting of her forehead and lips. We both stay like that for a long moment, holding each other without touching.

'You're the only thing I'll miss,' she says. 'I don't care where he takes us. But I'll miss you.'

And then she says something that makes my head so light it disconnects and floats off my neck.

'But you've got to know this: I'll never come back. I won't write or call. You think you will, but you're never going to see me again.'

I nod, keeping my eyes closed against the hot water that spills down my face, and take air in childish gasps. I had no idea I could cry like this. I didn't know you can cry and not stop, not want to stop.

* * *

I go on and finish high school without much event, passing the last year and a half in a blurry fever, a codeine haze. There's no desperation, I just slow down and don't talk much, keep to myself in the shady corners, not caring about growing up one way or the other. My memories are of time spent looking out of windows, listening to lawnmowers, barking dogs or passing snowploughs. I'm the kid at the back of class you never notice, never wonder about. You're not even sure you've ever heard my name.

Names. I'm right at the end and I didn't even tell you her name. Maybe I can't remember it now, not exactly. But some people like to know details like that. They need to know. Without a name they can't be sure if the person actually existed, if they ever really came together with them in some way, if they now belong to the facts or fiction of their lives.

Call Roxanne

WE PULL OVER at a service centre on the 401 just outside
Kingston. My father thinks it's best if we get gas now before
we head north on the two-lane highway towards Peterborough
because you never know when you'll come across a gas station
up there. He seems to think that everything outside Toronto
and north of the 401 is sparse woodland populated only by car-
nivorous blackflies, devious mechanics and even worse dan-
gers (are there bears this far south?) waiting to prey upon
unprepared motorists like us.

'We should get gas here,' my father says as he angles off the
highway into the service-centre lane. 'Just in case we have any
trouble.'

I think of those Saturday matinee TV westerns where the
bad guy forces a showdown with the sheriff in the saloon. The
good guy always says, 'I don't want no trouble!' But who does?
My father doesn't. I don't. But that's what I must be to him
now. An inconvenience, a sputtering engine, an interruption
of normalcy.

Trouble.

* * *

My father's taking me to a hospital. I'd prefer not to talk about
the place itself. They tell me it's good to describe all experi-
ences, there's something therapeutic in recollection, but I'm
not so sure that's true, so I'll leave the hospital part for some
other time. For now, I'm just remembering my father driving
me there.

The first thing you should know is that he drives in the
same way he does everything else. Carefully. His field of
vision stops at the painted lines that define the highway, sepa-
rates the flattened tar from the distractions of fence-bordered
fields or billboards. His head doesn't move. All my life on the
streets of the small town where we live he's passed me without stopping on his way home from work. I could wave, jump,
scream 'Look out!' from the curb and he would cruise right by,

his head and eyes held straight. There was nothing for me to do but stand and watch the car pass, my father's profile unmoving and square. Sometimes I would think he was ignoring me on purpose. But they tell me not to create false intentions, that that was just the way he drove, it's not a good idea to read into things too much. I have stolen peeks at my file. My list of symptoms includes mild paranoia.

* * *

While my father pumps the gas and checks the oil, I go into the restaurant to use the toilet. From the outside, the building is designed like the 1950s conception of what a flying saucer looks like: a huge aspirin with a single, spiky antenna on top. Inside there is a cafeteria offering hamburgers, fries and gravy, fruit juice circulating in clear plastic displays and a colourfully advertised daily special. Today it is meatloaf with mixed vegetables.

I go to the washroom and select a toilet: the last one, under the little ventilation window. I go in and close the door behind me, slide the latch over and lock myself in.

At first, I don't unzip or sit down or do anything. I'm reading the graffiti that covers the walls, silver scratches in the pea-green paint. There is so much there is now hardly any room to add to it except at the extreme lower corners. Messages, proclamations, political slogans, jokes, lewd pictures, invitations, secret codes. There are arrow-struck hearts containing initials and first names, praise for rock bands (LED ZEP RULES!) and even a shaky, hurried, seemingly desperate sketch of a penis. But what interests me the most are the messages that invite some kind of actual, personal contact. Mostly these are by men who don't leave their names but scribble scheduled times and places for others. There are phone numbers of women, too, accompanied by a recommendation:

FOR A GOOD SCREW, CALL LYDIA MITCHELL.
DEBBIE SUCKS HARD MEAT.
LAURIE BATTEN IS THE BEST FUCK AT QUEEN'S.
I wonder if these women know they are being advertised in

this way, that their names are even here, their fame being made through an advertisement of sexual accomplishment. Are they written by ex-boyfriends, travellers proud of local conquests, frustrated suitors? Are they lies?

There is one message that, for some reason, stays with me. It is simple, clearly written in calm, square letters. The name stands out with the familiarity of an established fact.

CALL ROXANNE – 954-5412.

There is no promise of a good time. The writing doesn't have the same harassed, nervous scrawl as the others. Maybe Roxanne is something entirely different: a faith healer, masseuse, a reader of tarot cards. Maybe she provides a less complicated service. You just call Roxanne and she's there for you, a friend who knows what's going on. A voice with many faces because everyone is forced to create her on their own.

As I leave, I glance at myself in the long mirror above the sinks. I almost expect something to indicate instability: a glazed, bloodshot stare, or an unconsciously crooked, maniacal grin. Instead, I look rested and healthy.

I go outside and head towards the car. My father's standing beside it fiddling with the windshield wipers, checking for wear and tear. I notice that, despite his age and bad back, he has good posture. He stands like a man whose work involves the lifting of things, and for a moment I forget what it is my father does for a living. Remember, and forget again.

* * *

I play with the radio. I'm not interested in the music or any organized sound. It's just good to hear the bits and pieces jumble together, separated by stabs of static. I turn the knob all the way to the right side, then all the way to the left, watch the red line run frantically behind the station numbers like something that is trapped.

'Leave that,' my father says without looking over, shaking his finger at the radio.

'What? Which part?'

'The station with the opera. The singing.'

He rolls his finger, motioning me to go back. I find it in a second: a crackly, hollow recording of a woman singing power-fully, accompanied only by a piano. The piano sounds far away, as if when they were recording it they put it at the back of the room and the microphone at the opposite end, hanging in the face of the singer.

The language isn't English, but it's clear that the message is tragic loss. Her voice trembles but never loses the note. It sounds like she's moving back and forth, as if swaying from the force of her efforts.

'There. That's it. Now, isn't that beautiful?' my father asks. He shifts in his seat, moves back, relaxes a little. It's as if this is what he's been waiting for all day, the relief of this woman, her voice and distant piano.

'She's very good. She sounds well-trained,' I say.

'Oh, yes. It's their *lives*. They work all their *lives* to sound like that.'

He nods, impressed by the conviction of her voice. I am too, but I can't bring myself to become a part of it. The experience of the singing is too selfish, a performance. Whatever emotion she's feeling is a creation that someone before her had written down on paper and now she was pretending it was hers alone.

When she is finished, an announcer comes on. He talks about the history of the piece and the biography of the singer herself. He is full of facts, knows everything about the empiri-cal, behind-the-scenes circumstances of that bit of music. After a while my father reaches over and turns the radio down to nearly nothing and opens his window halfway. He stares ahead, a captain peering into a gale.

'The engine's knocking a little,' he says.

* * *

As we drive I play with things in my head. I keep thinking of this one thing I know really happened. It has to do with what they did to Carlotta Matson.

It happened at school, when I was thirteen. Carlotta was two years older, pretty, with bleached, summertime blue eyes. She was popular too, in the way that detached, attractive people are. I never resented her for that, though. If I were a beautiful girl, I would be selective too.

Carlotta liked to hang around older people, sometimes a lot older. This is because she had a choice. She looked older than she was, and her body was developed in a way that made her seem like she could be any age. It was, at fifteen, her passport to the adult world.

She had boyfriends. Most had shadowy beards over their jawlines and drove pickup trucks with oversized tires. Farm boys. They drank beer in their trucks in the parking lot after school, leering at anyone who passed by, whistling like drunk strip-club patrons when Carlotta came down the path. She would get in with them, the music would be turned up, and the trucks would squeal and doughnut their way out. As they went, the boys would hoot out their windows, leaving a sandy, hanging dust in the air behind them.

Who knew where they went? Nobody could even guess at Carlotta's exotic world. It must have involved beer, farmfield joyrides and sex, but that's all I could guess at. After school I would watch them go and then walk home talking to myself, stepping on every crack in the sidewalk.

This is what I saw them do to Carlotta:

There are three trucks that afternoon, with boys lying on the hoods drinking cans of beer and passing a stubby bottle of Jack Daniel's around, taking off their shirts and sunning themselves like soldiers between raids. One of them walks around the trucks, slapping backs and giving hard, stagy handshakes. He is their leader, and everyone knows his name. Oddly, it looks like a French winemaker's name on paper (Louis Lamontagne) but we all pronounce it as though the name of an American cartoon character: *Lewy Lemontang*.

Carlotta comes out of school as usual, but when she sees Louis she hesitates. She walks toward him slowly, knowing something is about to be handed down, a scene made. She wears white shorts and a red tube-top, the kind of fleshy, tight-fitting thing that would not be worn today, having been replaced by other tight-fitting things. She looks small, even though she has the body and self-conscious, hip-rolling walk of a grown woman. It strikes me how smooth her skin looks, how tight, muscular and brown her thighs and legs are. She is an athletic and incidentally beautiful child.

Somehow everybody in the schoolyard knows something is about to happen. Without a word of warning, a crowd gathers. We're all watching Carlotta walk towards the truck as if she has to, as if it is her father or the principal there waiting for her.

Before a thing is said, Louis hits her. He takes his arm up as if he's about to point to the sky and shout but instead brings his hand down in a fist into her face. Carlotta falls to her knees and puts her hand to her nose and lips. Already there is blood everywhere: her shoulders, the pavement, her hands, a glistening paint on her white shorts.

Louis hits her again. This time he brings his hand down like a cleaver to the back of her neck as if he would chop it off. She rolls to the ground and pulls herself up into a ball. The only sounds are a combination of heavy metal (was it Deep Purple?) and Carlotta whimpering and gurgling, blowing the blood out her nose.

This is the part that stays with me:

Louis bends down and, in a second, straightens her body out on the parking lot gravel. He stretches her arms up, grabs her top and pulls it off. Then he unbuttons her shorts and pulls them down but not quite off, leaves them a torn circle around her ankles.

He stands back and looks at her. We all look at her. We stare. Nobody moves or speaks, nobody runs to get a teacher or call the police. In fact, it is a long time before anyone does a goddamn thing.

Whenever I think of Carlotta Matson now it seems it's for a reason. The reason has to do with the look on her face when she was left beaten and naked in the parking lot. She seemed to know there was some chain of events that had led to this, but she couldn't figure out the system of those events. She was more surprised than injured, as if the victim of a misunderstanding, or the brunt of a somewhat excessive practical joke.

I remember her and I want to say out loud, 'You see! There's another example!' But an example of what? That's what happened to Carlotta, just Carlotta. Not everybody is guilty of doing things like that to people.

But we watched. We were all watching, even if we weren't

actually there. And now I think I see Carlotta everywhere.

* * *

A few years ago my father had a heart attack. I was at school when it happened. My name was called over the P.A. and I had to go to the office. There the principal met me, with saggy eyes and wounded, responsible shoulders. His voice was heavy and rehearsed. I thought of him as a man who enjoyed living up to expectations of his professional capacity for understanding. When he told me what happened all I can remember is his puffy face, screwed up in exaggerated sympathy. I also remember how the words 'heart attack' echoed in my head. Two minutes ago I was in English class working on my *Midsummer Night's Dream* book report, and now the principal's damp, ashtray breath was blowing *heart attack* over my face and to my ears. At the time I believed the whole thing was set up as one of my psychological tests. This one was designed to see how I responded to spontaneous emotional crisis.

The principal drove me to the hospital. On the way to his car, he kept his arm carefully around my shoulders, as if there was a real threat of my collapsing. I was led that way to my father, who had been put in one of those complicated beds garnished by equipment with display screens and different coloured lights. Bags of liquid food and medicines hung on metal hangers, regularly dripping their contents into tubes which led into his arms, his blood. Things were stuck in him, taped to his chest, inserted down his throat. It looked as if these things came directly from him, growing from the inside out as bizarre, alien tumours.

I don't remember visiting him when his eyes were open. He was there for three weeks, and for all I knew he slept through it all. I would sit by his bed in a fold-out metal chair on the opposite side from the machines keeping him alive and stare at his face, wait for him to wake up or move or say something. It didn't feel right to sit there looking at my father without turning away. He would have told me that it's rude to stare. But I had nothing else to do. His grey face fell away in soft wrinkles from his nose, but his forehead, even up close, was still smooth. Breath passed softly through his lips, his mouth partly open in a childish oval. Under the single hospital sheet, his body settled as if being slowly absorbed by the mattress.

I would force myself to hold his hand, not because I thought it would do any practical good but because I saw other people doing it, sitting beside other sick people in their critical beds. His hand felt cold, doughy, pliant. It frightened me to think that if he died while I was there I would feel the life go out of him somehow. I imagined that his hand would jolt or squeeze mine, that there would be some last electrical signal or muscular reflex and then nothing.

I tried to remember ever holding his hand before, but came up only with pictures I'd seen of other people's families. Still, I didn't expect I could be as unfamiliar with something as plain and unhidden as my father's hand. It felt like I was breaking the rules by holding it, because I certainly wouldn't have if he was awake and well. It felt like I was cheating what we had set up with each other over the years and for no other reason than his coming close to death. Would he approve, even at a time like that, deviating from what we expected of each other? He would be embarrassed to know that our formalities, reserve and careful distance had been thrown away in a hospital, a place where those things should most be maintained. But I did it anyway, borrowing feelings from the death-bed scenes of American television.

Why couldn't I make this simple gesture real? I know it sounds awful, and I feel like shit saying it, but I felt guilty every time I held his hand when he was in that scientific bed. But I went on doing it, nodding thoughtfully at the nurses when they came by to fill something up or take something away. I did it like the other visitors on the critical ward who felt it was important to hold a hand and not just sit and watch as if you were really just waiting for something horrible to happen.

* * *

As we drive north, the machine-organized, mathematical fields give way to forest. Though we see none, signs warn us of deer crossing. With the window down, the car is filled with smells, one blending with and following the other as we pass its source: pine needles, mustard weed, skunk. It feels good to be near these things.

I play with the idea that I am one day going to meet Roxanne. By now, she has become more than a name and a number, she has entered the world of my false memory. We've had arranged meetings, long talks in quiet places about ourselves. We speak of why we are who we are. She tells me secrets, and I tell her about beautiful places I'd like to one day see. She likes me. She tells me this herself.

In my mind, we have had a life together, but the events of that life are still distant and vague.

I'm still creating them.

* * *

My father walks me up to my room at the hospital. He follows behind, climbing the stairs with irregular, difficult, arthritic stomps. What I took earlier to be good posture must have been a mistake made from the distance, a lucky angle. Now he looks stooped, his shoulders and neck rounded, unsupported, caving in to his chest. He's getting older. 'We're all getting older,' he would say to that, without any particular sadness.

My room is large. It has three big windows that form a semi-circle at one end, opposite the bed. I walk over to them, and I sense my father waiting in the doorway behind me. Maybe he wants to give me a little privacy, a chance to get used to the new surroundings. Maybe he waits because he doesn't want to come in, it might delay this whole procedure and he can't wait to get the hell out of here. I don't blame him. All hospitals have that bleached odour of things not being right.

From the windows I can see the front drive lined symmetrically with tall, carefully pruned pine trees, so perfect they look fake. In the middle of the broad front lawn is a stone fountain, full of cherubs holding bunches of grapes and huge bowls on their shoulders. A woman with long hair and a sympathetic smile stands in the centre, lifting a wine jug that perpetually spills its contents back to where it came from. She looks completely unconcerned that if it were real wine she'd be making a terrible mess.

I turn around and my father is still there. He hasn't entered the room, he has decided to create a threshold. This is my room, in my hospital. He stays out of it because this is a place of science and he's not qualified.

'Are you going to be all right? I'm sure we've forgotten something, but I can bring it up later if you really need it,' he says, bringing things to a close. I'm here now, among professionals, there's nothing more he can do. Besides, what's the point in a long goodbye?

'I'll be fine,' I say, sounding fairly certain.

He nods, in a way that says that everything, according to some plan that is impossible to understand, will work itself out.

Finally he turns and goes, giving me a little wave when his back is turned. He's at the top of the stairs, his hand on the railing to steady himself for the descent, and I suddenly feel I have to say something to him. I owe him some words to let him know I wish he didn't have to go through this, to deal with a son with mechanical problems.

'Dad!'

He turns, not expecting anything. *Did you leave your toothbrush in the car?* his eyes ask.

'Thanks for the ride,' I say.

He gives another little wave. *No problem*, it says. *It's the least I can do. I'm your father.*

As he goes down the stairs, his head lowering with each step, I wonder why I can't say more. I thanked him as if he were nothing more than a driver who's given a hitchhiker a lift. Did he know I meant something larger than that? You could never be sure with him, or with anyone really, but I hope so. I hope he can understand me and all the troublesome things in my head without either of us having to say a word.

I watch his head descend, my right hand in my pocket, rolling and folding a single slip of paper. It is no larger than a pack of matches, but it fills my hand.

On it is Roxanne's number.

If You Lived Here You'd Be Home By Now

MY FATHER MARKETED oil filters, played softball, drank Blue and wasn't a bad guy until he remarried and accepted Jesus as his Saviour. This idea was planted in his head by Beth, my stepmother, who effortlessly convinced him of the existence of God by replacing McCain's frozen lasagne with pot roast and *Penthouse* wanks with a missionary session once a week after *Hockey Night in Canada*. Within three months I turned eighteen, Beth moved in, 'Rules of the House' were posted on the fridge, and enough crosses were nailed over windows and door frames to make living in Salem's Lot feel safe. My father, the one I knew before he gave his life over to a Higher Authority, was gone. He wasn't crazy, just converted, walking around behind Beth with a slack, eager-to-please expression buttered over his face. For a time they tried to get me, too, but I closed my ears, smiled, nodded, and recited Smiths lyrics in my head.

This went on until somewhere in the middle of grade thirteen when I went AWOL. I was a runaway, but only in that I had *run away*, and not in the sense that anyone was going to come after me or call the cops or put my picture on milk cartons above a 1-800 number. I packed a single duffel bag, took my father's bank card out of his wallet, left a note on the fridge and moved to the city from the town I grew up in, where 'town' is used to describe a collection of streets radiating out from the perpendicular meeting of two dead-straight, two-lane highways. One went east to Toronto and west to Lake Huron, the other went south to Lake Erie and north to Who-Cares-Where. There was a feed co-op, a mini-mall, a hockey arena and a high school because there had to be a place to bus the farmers' kids until they turned sixteen and lined up for jobs at factory openings or jumped on the tractor to plough under the rest of their days.

The Greyhound arrived in Toronto at three, so I figured I had until dinner to find a place to live. I picked up one of the alternative weeklies stuck under a seat in the waiting room, turned to the classifieds, and ripped out the first ad I came to. It didn't appear under Rooms for Rent, but Help Wanted:

Body needed to occupy small space and surrender $270 every 30 days. Life sustaining protection from the elements provided in exchange. The Inexperienced (you know who you are) need not apply. Call 537-5313 (The Project) and ask for Dixon if untroubled by pandemonium, stench, periodic cannibalism and glimpses into the Void.

The phone rang fourteen times before anyone answered (I was prepared to go to twenty) and then it was a male voice, exhaling smoke. '*Buenos dias.*'
'Is this The Project?'
'Is this the applicant?'
'Yes.'
'Across from Grange Park. I'll be conducting interviews all day. I won't need to give you the precise address.'
It took directions from four panhandlers and two hours to get from the bus station to Grange Park, just north of Queen. The Project – what must have been The Project – was the only house on the block painted to look like a face, with silver eyelashes made of twisted up aluminum foil over the second floor windows, cherry cheeks on the brick beneath them, and a front door white with grinning teeth. The door was opened by a skinny guy wearing tartan boxers and an ABBA T-shirt. He was my age, but with two enormous black pouches resting heavily on his cheekbones.
'Hi. I'm here about the room.'
'What's wrong with the room?'
'Nothing. I'm here about *renting* the room.'
'Oh. That's not my job,' he said. 'Dixon interviews all the applicants.'
'So there's a lot of people ... a lot of applicants?'
'No. You're the first. *Dixon!*'
In a few seconds a short guy with a goatee dyed a perfect red came to the door.
'I'm Dixon,' he said, crumbs exploding out of his mouth. He was eating a Pop Tart stuck between two slices of bread. 'This

tall fellow is Sid. I suppose you want to look at the room first.'
I stepped in and Sid loped off down the front hallway, leaving me alone with the red goatee.
'Are you into anything?' he asked me.
'Yeah. You know. No. What do you mean, exactly?'
'You know: filmmaking, a band ...'
'No. I'm a writer.'
That was that. Never written anything I hadn't been absolutely forced to aside from my father's signature on report cards but there I was saying it. *I'm a writer.* Who knew where it came from, or whether it was based on anything more than the feeling that I had to say something, that I had to be *into* something to live this close to Queen Street, or whether it was a deeply felt desire that had risen abruptly to the surface after the hypnotist clicked his fingers. No matter what the story on that is, as soon as I said it there was an immediate and convincing ring of truth about it, as I suppose is the case with all well-told lies.
'A writer. What do you write there, Hemingway?'
'Episodes. I'm into episodes. Thinking about putting them together sometime. But right now it's the episodes I'm into.'
'Well, that makes two of us. Grab your shit. Your room's on the third floor. If you get in here at night and can't find the light switch just keep going up until you walk into a pitch black, ice cold, threatening space. That'll be your room.'

★ ★ ★

The house was a detached on Beverley Street, close enough to Queen that the sounds of wasted club-goers could be heard with increasing volume as the week progressed: scattered hoots on Monday and Tuesday, group shouts and a couple shattered bottles on Wednesday, squealing tires, squealing girls, and the smell of weed on Thursday, *boom-boom* car speakers and dumb-guy profanities Friday and Saturday, and then funereal calm on Sunday when the streets were occupied only by yuppies returning north from their groovy downtown brunches. All of this, the cycle of the city, could be seen and heard from the single, compact window of my bedroom, which was not a bedroom at all but half a bedroom, the second half lying on the other side of an erected piece of drywall that muffled sound with the effectiveness of newspaper. In the other half lived someone the others called Bass (pronounced like the fish, not the musical instrument). He had a girlfriend who stayed over most nights and other girlfriends who stayed over on the nights she didn't, such that he was never alone. Yet the noise that passed through the veil of plaster that separated our spaces was not what you'd expect of two people having sex, but of one man, Bass, stating, 'Take off your clothes,' and then silence. It was always the same. Just him, and no floor-squeaking to suggest anything more. Whatever he did with himself and those women in that room did not involve speech or physical movement of any kind, but I was jealous just the same, knowing that, unlike me, at least he wasn't alone.

I didn't have the money or the friends to go out so I stayed in and tried to write, out of boredom at first and then out of a sense of obligation that I had to do something to support the bold and ridiculous claim I had made to Dixon on the day I moved in. There wasn't too much thought about what I wrote. It was satisfying enough that when someone else in the house passed by my door and looked in I could be seen half-wrapped in the single blanket on my bed, writing in unused U. of T. exam booklets that Sid had found in a recycling bin on Spadina, using a pen that someone at some point had taken from a room at the Royal York. It was the kind of behaviour that I supposed suggested a portrait-of-the-artist-as-a-young-man thing. At any rate, anyone who bothered to take a look in on me appeared to be satisfied.

There were parties, but it was impossible to tell the parties from every other night a bunch of messed-up people happened to be sitting around. These people could be broken down into five basic groups: the Musicians, the Artists, the Filmmakers, the Actors, and the Hangers-on. There were no Writers. It didn't seem enough to base an identity on. That's why I was a Hanger-on.

So whether there was a party going on or not, there was always somebody sitting on the single sofa in the living room, smoking or rolling or tripping or explaining a great idea they'd had for a short film. Everyone had these wry anecdotes they thought could be turned into great short films. Some actually were produced, funded by rare university or government grants or, more usually, neglectful and guilt-ridden uptown parents. Many were shot at The Project, and the day of the shoot was always sort of exciting, on account of the lights and shouts of 'Action!' and 'Cut!' and actresses showing their breasts, for most of these films somehow or other involved women showing their breasts.

When the film was developed and edited (which happened to about one out of every three – the editing process seemed to take the interest out of the most interesting ideas) they would be screened at the house. Invitations would be photocopied and handed out at parties and bars the week before, home-made posters plastered wherever other posters were plastered. Then people would show up for the 'launch' – and when the lights went down and the projector started up I would stand at the back of the room and nod my head if anyone looked my way, put my finger to my lips in a gesture of deep thought, and imagine this ten-minute, black-and-white, incomprehensible thing on the screen being literally launched into existence, beamed into space like those radio transmissions that are meant as a signal to aliens on other planets but that for all any-one knows may never be picked up at all.

*　*　*

I didn't call home for three weeks. When I did I was expecting fire and brimstone, but instead got resignation and fatigue.

'We've been looking all over for you, son.'

'Really? Where?

'What?'

'Where have you looked?'

'You know.... We've looked in our hearts.'

'You could've tried directory assistance.'

We were both quiet for a while, then I told him I was sorry about stealing his bank card.

'Well, it's no good any more. I changed the PIN number on it.'

'I know.'

After that we talked for a while, and it wasn't too bad. He spoke of the miserable win/loss record of his industrial league hockey team, blaming it all on the goalie whose blindness in one eye prevented him from seeing shots from the left wing. I complained about Kraft Dinner as a breakfast substitute. God wasn't mentioned. But after I hung up I realized that he never asked me if I was OK, if I needed any money, or when I was planning on coming home.

* * *

My out-of-doors time was spent heading down to the corner store and returning with a can of soup or a loaf of Bambi bread, thinking: *This is home.* Then I'd remember this billboard on the 401 I would see with my father when he'd take me to Toronto to buy stuff you couldn't get at the mall in town. It was stuck on a manmade hill that was meant to block the sound of traffic from the monster homes on the other side whose chimneys, always smokeless, rose up like periscopes over the crest. The billboard was meant to provoke the sorry commuters who must have had to pass it every day from even further-flung, cheaper 'communities'. The slogan, painted over an artist's sketch of a fake-Tudor, 2,400-square-foot thing that presumably lay on the other side, was a taunt to all others who had a ways to go yet:

IF YOU LIVED HERE YOU'D BE HOME BY NOW

'That doesn't make sense,' my father would say. 'If I lived there, I wouldn't be *home*, I'd just be living in a different *house*.'

Maybe this has to do with leaving home and my father finding Jesus and growing up in a town of losers, but this is my theory: home is always somewhere else. It's like we're all perpetual commuters heading one way and then turning around and going back, on and on forever. And along the way we look into windows and see other people stirring pots in cluttered kitchens, discovering a new wrinkle in the mirror over the mantel, lifting pizza to mouths in the blue glow of the TV. You think that if you lived in any of those places, if you were those people, you'd be home by now. But you're probably not. Not them. Not home yet.

I explained my theory to Dixon.

'You're assuming people *want* to go home,' he said.

* * *

I wrote something – a short story about a promiscuous lesbian who turns out to be a straight male cross-dresser who can't get erections with women unless he dresses as one – and had it published in *Piss Pot*, a literary pamphlet distributed in free stacks sitting at the end of Queen Street bars. For two weeks this raised my profile to the level of occasional public recognition ('Hey! You live at The Project, right? Wrote that dyke thing in the *Pot*? Hilarious!') and when Dixon saw it he came up to my room and took me out to buy me a drink.

'Did you read it? What did you think?' I asked him, expecting praise.

'I don't read, Hemingway. I mean I *can*, and I used to pretend I *did*, but I *don't*.'

'At least you're honest.'

'Occasionally. Just don't ask me to read it. I would be tempted to tell you what I honestly thought of it.'

He took me to La Hacienda, a narrow burrito place lit only by candles stuck in old beer bottles.

'There's a big party tomorrow night at The Project. I think you should come,' Dixon said, his eyebrows joined above his nose with concern. It was a face I guessed was borrowed from his father.

'I live there. Do I need to be invited?'

'No, no, of course not. It's just that you never come out of your fucking room, so I thought you might have been *waiting* for an invitation. You're an odd duck, Hemingway. Some of us have assumed you're *intense*. But my guess is you're shy.'

'I'm neither. Thanks for the invite.'

We went out the sliding door at the back onto what in warmer weather must have been the patio, but the weather was not warm, and by the time Dixon had pulled a joint out of his vest pocket, found a match and lit it, our hands were frozen white candlesticks in the dark. Dixon inhaled once and passed it over to me, rolling it from his index finger to mine in the way potsmokers pass joints to others.

'One thing about you, Hemingway. You think about the future. Most of the people I hang with – we're present, PRESENT, *PRESENT*. But you're not about that, are you?'

'I don't know.'

'You're actually *doing* it. The artist's life. Writing, getting in *Piss Pot*, staying in your room. You don't talk, you *do*.'

'I think you might be wrong there. For example, I need to find a job, and I haven't done a fucking thing about that.'

'Job, yes, but I mean art. We talk about art all the time: media this, culture that. We *talk* about *art*. I could talk your small-town head off about Goings On about Town, Hemingway, but the thing is there's not much Goings On about Me.'

'That's good … "not much Goings On about Me"….'

I handed the joint back to him, now a char-shrivelled nib, and I realize I've smoked most of it on my own, and remind myself not to be so selfish with drugs if offered any at the party the next night.

'No, it's not good. I think about it sometimes. It sounds weird to say it – a twenty-one-year-old man – but I think that I may never do what I want to do.'

'What do you want to do?'

'Specifically? I'm not certain. But I know what it *involves*. Avoiding certain things. Making something true, something that cuts through all the shit. Something that I have *made* that is *better* than me. Like your story.'

'But you didn't read my story.'

'You know what I mean.'

Dixon took a final haul off the roach and inhaled it straight out of his numb fingers and into his mouth, and from the angle where I stood I could see the glowing red end bounce off his tonsils, extinguish, and fall down his throat.

'Fuck!'

'Are you all right?'

'Fine. More scar tissue, that's all. More wounds that won't heal.'

'You have a dramatic way about you, Dixon. You should act, you know that?'

He raised his eyes to mine and laughed, and his mouth emitted a single, comical puff of smoke.

'I'm trying, Hemingway! I'm *trying!*'

★ ★ ★

The morning of the day of the party I got a letter from my father. There was something from Beth too, a matchbook-sized prayer book with 'Read This, for the Love of Christ' written over a picture of Jesus' blood-streaked face on the front. My father's letter was written on his company's stationery, which had an oil filter floating on a puffy cartoon cloud in the right-hand corner.

Dear Son,

Thought I'd write to let you know that me and Beth are well. In fact it was her idea that I write this letter, to let you know that we've made some decisions at our end about things.

I've prayed for you, but not all prayers are answered. Grace isn't that easy. And you'll find that life isn't that easy.

But there are lessons in suffering. That's what we're learning about right now in family counselling. We've learned that loving your children sometimes means turning away, so that the wickedness of the world may be shown to them, and they may finally find God or choose the path to Damnation for themselves. So good luck.

I won't be writing or calling again for a while. Me and Beth think it's the right thing to do. They call it Tough Love, but like Beth said to me, 'Just think of it as Love.'

Dad

P.S. Please don't call collect. It's part of the programme – and it upsets Beth when the phone bill comes in.
P.P.S. Our goalie is losing sight in his good eye now. I guess winning isn't everything!

I thought of symbolic ways of destroying it, but in the end stuck it up on the wall in my room. The letter hung there alone on the bare whiteness like an exhibit at a modern art gallery. The strange thing about it was that the words you could make out first when you stepped toward it were 'Son' and then 'Grace' and then 'God'. A lot of people later found that mysterious and cool – the way some kind of Holy Trinity came out at you from my father's scrawled text. I could never decide whether to find these comments funny or sad.

* * *

The party started that night with a single rush of people, as though they'd all been waiting outside and then decided to break down the door. Instantly they clogged the space in the kitchen before anywhere else. The kitchen was large but one corner was occupied by a cone of garbage bags that had been left long enough to develop an oozing black syrup around its perimeter. The odour in the room was a complicated combination of decay and perfume, but together it reminded me of the Essex County Abattoir. My father and I used to have to drive past it on our way to the landfill outside of town to dump off an old mattress or Christmas tree, and he would tell me to plug my nose but it would do no good. 'They're sure killing the little piggies today!' he would shout, as though this fact marked a special occasion. The smell didn't seem to bother him, and when we got home he would make us bacon sandwiches for dinner.

Everyone drank Sid's homebrew out of coffee mugs because it was free and there weren't any glasses. Nothing but Sid's brown suds, which looked a little too much like the bubbles that form on the surface of toxic ponds they show on the news every once in a while. And there was something about it that caused every swallow to be a struggle against gagging. I got a mug for myself and stood in the kitchen along with everyone else until I noticed this girl standing next to the stove. She was smiling, or at least had been smiling and just stopped. Whichever it was there was something sweet about her face, in the way a trace of a smile seemed to be there even though she wasn't smiling at that particular moment. After I made my way through the scrum I leaned against the stove beside her, my eyes down at my feet now stuck in the gooey moat of the garbage pile.

'Do you ever feel like dust? A piece of dust?' I asked after a while.

'No.'

'I mean, it's like, imagine – imagine you were once attached to something – a scalp, say – somebody's scalp – and then this someone scratches its head and that's it. You used to be part of somebody's skin, and now you're dust, and you're just drifting, waiting to settle on a coffee table or get tangled up in a spider's web – but it doesn't matter, no matter where you end up, because you're just a piece of dust?'

She looked at me with her mouth partly open and her eyebrows lifted and the sweetness – what I thought might have been sweetness – was gone.

'Is that the best you can do?' she said.

She lifted her mug of toxic froth to her lips, walked away into the crowd and did not look back. If she had stayed I would have said yes. That's about the best I can do.

I stayed there until Bass, who up until that moment had never spoken to me outside of a morning grunt passing between turns at the toilet, now approached me and smiled.

'Hemingway.'

'Yeah.'

'How's it goin'?'

'Good. OK.'

'Cool.'

For a time we said nothing, and I watched him nod his head at me as if in agreement. Then he said, 'Wanna do x?'

'Yes. Please.'

'Cool.'

He extended his hand and in the centre sat a single tablet. I picked it up and swallowed it on the instant gush of saliva in my mouth.

Bass kept nodding and I realized I was nodding along with him. From across the room we would have looked like two old friends recalling a familiar truth. I wanted to say something, but Bass's presence seemed to discourage words. When he finally moved past me and shimmied himself through the clog of bodies toward the kitchen I thought, and may have even said aloud, 'There goes a strange and fine man.'

'Hem-ing-way!'

Dixon was upon me. And although his arrival was the next thing I remembered, it may have been an hour before he did. My time was being spent experiencing the pleasure of standing absently among strangers.

'Yes. It's me.'

'So does this rank as a worthy episode?'

'It does.'

'Bass told me you were tripping.'

'Bass is a strange and fine man.'

'If you say so. Shit, man. You look a little green. Grab your beer, we'll get some air.'

We went out the back door and into the alley. It didn't feel cold, but fat snowflakes tumbled out of the black sky and made everything quiet, even the music from inside, which was now just a bass drum thumping through the wall. Dixon lit a cigarette and took a long, hungry drag before speaking.

'Are you going home for Christmas?'

'Is it Christmas?'

'Day after tomorrow.'

'I didn't know. I need to get out more.'

'You need to watch TV more.'

I took another swallow of the home brew and felt again the gag reflex seize my throat as it descended. Then we both stood under the sickly orange of the alley streetlight and let the snow collect on our shoulders and heads, listened to the cabs slush through the street around the corner. We said nothing to each other, as friends allow themselves to do with friends.

I stood there and thought about everything I had and did not have in the world. No job, forty-six dollars, a duffel bag of T-shirts and paperbacks, a cancelled bank card, a Jesus freak for a father and the growing idea in my head that nothing from here on in would be anything like what had come before.

I was terribly happy.

Kiss Me

JASMINE BROADHURST. First name like department store perfume and last name like a street. They say you always remember losing your virginity but I don't, not really. But I do remember the first time Jasmine Broadhurst transferred the gum in her mouth into mine, without warning, guiding it in with a tender flick of tongue. It was the loveliest thing, something new inside of me, a warm lump of strawberry rubber. So artificially flavoured and excessively sweet it didn't even pretend to taste like fruit, but somehow it wasn't too bad when worn down by the spit of the one you love. And her eyes too close to my own to look at them both at the same time so I move back and forth between them and try to express something deep straight into her pupils. And the whole time I know I'm kissing her, *kissing* her. Jasmine Broadhurst. The first person to teach me that some things that sound unpleasant are fantastic when you just relax and let them happen.

After what's happened, Jasmine Broadhurst stands not for love but for the memory of love. Not so much the memory of the thing itself, but the feeling that it's possible, inevitable, a right. The pleasure in fooling yourself by borrowing serious feelings without the burden of carrying them with you for real. The comfort that there will always be someone else to kiss you, somewhere down the line, no matter what. But my face, the way it looks now, shows how wrong this assumption is. Even with eyes closed you can feel its ugliness. To kiss me would be to taste the metallic sourness of mottled scars. The rough edge of an empty soup tin.

I am repulsive. That's a hell of a thing to say to yourself every day. I know it from seeing my face reflected in others', the way the edges of their mouths drop and then tremble back up to an awkward mask of indifference. I see it in their bulging eyes as they recall what vampires look like in the movies when they are finally exposed to the sun.

I am the face you turn from on the street because it's rude

to stare, but you turn back to anyway, to feel again how lucky you are to live in the skin that you have. I appear in nightmares, bearing down with a crooked, open mouth and tongue moving around inside like a lizard in its hole. In this story I have made for myself I am the troll who lives under the bridge, sniffling in the shadows, closing my ears to the clamour of love as it passes over my head.

* * *

I burned my face lighting our third floor balcony barbecue.

It was the sort of day that provided no hints that a horrible disfiguration was about to happen: bright, a light breeze swirling up St. Urbain from the river, the Haitian kids on the ground floor sitting behind an upturned grapefruit crate selling plastic cups of lemonade. The little girl shouting 'C'est frais! It's cold!' every couple of minutes.

It was the lighting fluid. Crazy stuff, it really goes up. It was my habit to douse the hell out of the coals before lighting them so, when lit, they could dazzle your audience with a thrilling *whhooosshhh* and a short-lived bonfire that broiled cheeks from ten feet away. Another fun thing was to spray more fluid on when the flames were lowering to blaze it up again, aiming the can into the barbecue like a flamethrower. This is the dangerous part, there's even a warning against it on the label if you read the print below the little picture of an explosion. The problem is this: sometimes the flame follows the trail of fluid up towards the can like a lit fuse, and if you don't cut off the stream somehow you find yourself holding a live Molotov cocktail. When it blows, the fluid remaining in the can goes everywhere. For whatever reason on this particular occasion (being in flames I can't recall the exact physics involved) most of it ended up splashing over my face, dripping down my chin and over the tender part of my neck. I kept my eyes open and I remember the yellow flash and the black smoke rising off my skin before the heat melted off my eyelashes and seared my eyelids into half-shut slits.

I was conscious the whole time, flapping my hands over my face and, when the flames had gone out, opening the screen door and telling Leah to call an ambulance. I didn't scream, focusing all of my energy on breathing in regular intervals. But the pain was something I'd rather not describe, aside from saying it was what I imagine insanity to be like: consuming, relentless, a world entirely apart from the one you were born into.

Leah was pretty calm too, but in the way that people who are terrified become calm. After she got off the phone she came out the door carrying a glass of water. (Was this meant to put out the flames or quench my thirst?) When she looked at me she made a sound somewhere between a gasp and a gag but carefully bent down to set the glass on the floor. She said nothing but kept her eyes on me, her pupils the size of dimes in the bright sunshine.

'Do I have any hair?' I asked her.

'Not a lot.'

'It stinks. Burnt hair stinks.'

She gave me a look that said that bad smells should be the last of my worries. 'You're bleeding.'

'Am I?'

'Does it hurt?'

'Yes.'

'Oh, baby.'

Then she put her arm around my back and moved beside me on the tiny Juliet balcony to wait for the ambulance. It was during this time that I learned it's true what people in these situations always say: *The seconds felt like hours*.

'They'll be here soon,' she said.

'Fucking barbecue. We were going to have a *barbecue*,' I kept saying as we waited on the paint-flaky wood, holding each other in the sun. From a distance we would have looked like a couple making up after a fight, or consoling each other after receiving bad news.

* * *

When I was in the hospital Leah came to visit every day, sometimes twice, so that it seemed that when I wasn't knocked out on the dope they pumped into me she was always there. Even when the nurses came to change my bandages. A disgusting ritual. Three times a day layers of what used to be skin were removed and, slowly, the hardened ridges of my new face dried, thickened, emerged. Leah was there for all of it, watching. She was strong as hell, didn't flinch, but didn't go overboard on the sympathy either. Just stood there at the side of the bed and watched, taking my hand when I held it out. 'Oh, baby,' she'd say. 'What are we going to do with you?'

We had moved in together at the beginning of that summer. The plan was that this move was the beginning of a complete life together. Finish degrees, work for a while, save, travel, attend other people's weddings, find careers we could live with, children. We were at the stage of actually talking about all of this out loud. We saw ourselves as separate from the relationships our friends were in, distinguished by our degree of frankness, pragmatism, and talent. I spoke seriously of feelings and intentions that, if said to any woman before her, would have made me feel foolish, unsophisticated, an anxious farm boy going crazy after the first good sex of his life.

In the hospital Leah never told me how bad I looked. They kept me well away from mirrors and (intentionally, I think) served my food with plastic cutlery and juice in ceramic mugs. Nothing that could reflect myself back at me. I have since learned that more than the preservation of vanity or good spirits is at stake in such manoeuvres. In fact, burn victims have been known to go into long and untreatable shock when shown their faces too early. The doctors had spoken to Leah about this, and she was careful to look me directly in the eye, her blinking disciplined into consistency. She was cheerful, too, but never lied to me. Everybody else that drummed up the courage or guilt to visit dropped off magazines and lied their asses off, and who could blame them? But Leah never played down the situation if asked directly, which I rarely did, having had the question sufficiently answered the first time.

'So am I the Elephant Man, or more Phantom of the Opera?'

'The best parts of each.'

One night when I was in a particularly pissy mood because they had taken away the IV full of the good stuff and put me on the puny distraction of maximum dosage Tylenol-3, I became weepy. More than weepy: I bawled, screeched, blubbered, choked. I cried from the pain, but also for how the rest of my life would be diminished, how nothing would ever be as simple or privileged. Leah was there, crying along with me, asking the nurses for more dope and being told they didn't have the authority.

'I won't leave you,' she said, over and over.

At first I thought she meant *tonight*. *I won't leave you tonight before you get to sleep*. But the way she kept saying it, the intensity in her voice, made me realize she meant *after this*. *I won't leave you for being burned*. And even though she meant nothing but comfort in saying this, it struck me for the first time that such an event was a reasonable possibility. That she might *want* to leave me after this, that people have left others for similar reasons.

Leah was granting me the intimate favour of subtlety. Speaking about something without mentioning it directly, knowing it should be unnecessary to spell certain unpleasant thoughts out. She was reminding me of what I'd known all along from other people's lives but had yet to recognize as a possibility in my own: that, even under conditions of love, there are some events that change the rules entirely.

* * *

Leah's sympathy was not learned from the bedside scenes of daytime television. She knew something herself of how the failures of the body can get in the way of the anticipated patterns of life. That's why her presence at the hospital didn't embarrass or irritate me as it would if she were any other woman I've ever thought I could live with forever.

When Leah was twenty-two, before we met, she was the star of the university gymnastic team. I remember reading about her in the *McGill Daily*'s sports section where there was a buzz about her inclusion on the Canadian Olympic team. All of this was interrupted abruptly during a pre-dawn practice when her chalked feet missed the beam. As she fell her knee slammed against it, wrenching her leg out of its hip socket. The immediate pain brought her to the edge of unconsciousness but did not quite push her over. Instead, it induced hallucinations of puppets. The coaches and ambulance attendants who jostled over her took the form of wobbly marionettes controlled by a complex web of strings, their joints hinged on loose screws that threatened to come apart altogether. When they picked her up and placed her on the stretcher she could see strings attached to her own slack limbs, each one drifting up high into the gymnasium ceiling floodlights. The coach told her later that she kept asking 'Who's up there?' the whole time. She wanted to know who had failed her, who the puppet master was. Her question carried the stinging tone of betrayal: this whole thing was someone else's fault. She squinted up to see where all the strings led, but whoever controlled their movements was washed out in spheres of halogen light.

I met Leah shortly after her life had been changed by her vision of puppets. By that time the Olympics were over, and she would be too old by the time they came around again. Best-case scenarios now spoke of being able to walk one day without a noticeable limp, of scars that could be covered with black nylons or make-up when she wanted to wear a skirt. I was her boyfriend for the recovery period, going along for the visits to doctors, physiotherapists, consultations with ortho-paedic surgeons who showed us menacing plastic hip joints and stainless steel knees. Instead of kisses over St. Denis café tables or walks in Parc Mont-Royal, we spent a lot of time sit-ting in out-patient waiting rooms holding hands.

Through all of this Leah was brave, where 'brave' means covering your disappointment and anger with an ironic laugh and fatalistic shrug. It wasn't this alone that made me love her (can it ever be one thing?) but it was a part of it. I felt she was stronger than me, that all of this was a test that she was uniquely able to meet. When we made love Leah showed her scars, distorted angles and withered muscles with something close to pride, a womanliness. More than just making do with what you have, she turned the worst thing in her life into a claim of self-worth that went deeper than having straight and nearly Olympian legs.

* * *

Before, I used to daydream about breasts and legs and but-tocks. Leah's body. Touching these places with my hands. Leah leading me into rooms, smile heavy with suggestion, fingers unbuttoning things. Now it's lips. Not sex, but tender, eyes-open kisses. When I became ugly I stopped dreaming of physical vigour, and wished instead for the restrained tremors of delicacy. Or at least this is how I rationalized the fact that Leah and I weren't sleeping together any more. I took her invitations as charity, a gesture meant to bring me back into life. Desire, the simple wanting my body close to hers, had been ruled out.

'What's wrong?' she asks, her hand high on my thigh under the sheets.

'Please. Do we have to *talk* about it?'

'Just tell me what you'd like.'

My life back. No, not my life. Give *me* back.

'Don't serve me.'

'I'm not.'

'I'm sorry –'

'It's all right, it's all right.'

She holds me, buries her face in my neck. I almost tell her that I'm not sorry about anything except that she has to be here, now, with me, instead of someplace else where you don't need to feel embarrassed about a fucking thing.

* * *

Classes started again in the fall but I rarely showed up. Instead, I meticulously worked through the pile of magazines left for me at the hospital, reading *GQ* and *People* with the same careful attention as *Saturday Night* and the *New Republic.* I took to making messes, leaving stains, garbage and layers of clothing around the place. Made anxious by the idea of the grocery store's fluorescent lights, I stopped cooking altogether and relied on cheeseburgers supplemented by styrofoam tubs of *poutine.* I was fending for myself, a child left alone for the weekend, gorging on undeserved treats. Leah (whom I once loved to please with favourite meals) was left to warm tins of Habitant pea soup abandoned by the junkie couple who lived in the apartment before we moved in. By then it was the middle of winter, dark by five, and we ate in front of the TV with the lights off.

'You don't have to go *completely* to hell, you know,' Leah

tells me on her way out the bedroom door in the morning.

'It's not hell. Consider it a lifestyle choice.'

'Walk with me to school? You don't even have to go yourself. Just walk to the gates, turn around, and come straight home. It's called exercise.'

'No, it's called being patronized.'

'What do you want from me?'

'What have I asked you for?'

She pauses in the door frame, engulfed in instantaneous shafts of sunlight. Like Nosferatu, I raise my arm from the crypt to shield my eyes.

'I think we should get counselling,' she says.

'Oh. We've come to that. How long could we go before counselling was suggested? She thinks we should get counselling.'

'Please don't refer to me in the third person. That really pisses me off. I'm right here.'

'Right, OK. Then who should we call? 1-800-BURN VICTIM?'

Leah looks at me with her eyes set and square, willing herself to keep looking to prove she is not afraid. I look back at her as long as I can, but I am always the first to drop my eyes. Since the hospital I've caught enough Halloween flashes of myself in mirrors, silver kettles and polished knives to know exactly what she sees when she looks at me. It is the face of bad luck, and it looks back at her, blinks, tries to smile.

'I love you,' she says.

'Don't.'

'Don't what?'

'Just don't.'

She blows me a kiss and leaves. Holds her palm flat before her chin, kisses the air and exhales through her perfectly round mouth. I imagine it, tangible and warm, travelling in my direction through the space of the bedroom. But it must have missed me, because although I raise my head to meet it, I feel only the cool disturbance caused by the closing of the bedroom door.

* * *

'Kiss me,' she said and closed her eyes, just like Tina Louise from *Gilligan's Island* when she wanted to seduce somebody into rescuing her from the clumsy, numbskull castaways she got stuck with. Jasmine Broadhurst. A strange name compared to those of the other girls. Smelled a little strange, too. A combination of lemon deodorant and insect repellent, but this wasn't entirely bad. In fact I liked the way it prickled and made her seem sharp and tangy instead of the flowery bundles of *potpourri* the rest of them suggested.

'Kiss me,' she said, just like that, the strawberry gum lurking in her molars.

Love, was that it? Was that the feeling that moistened the eyes, sent gentle currents through the discs of the spine? No, not love, just a kiss outside the Stratford Arena in December, the Junior B team playing their Friday night game inside. Fourteen years old and nowhere else to go to stay warm. The smell of cherry Chap-Stick and father-borrowed splashes of musk Lectricshave on the collar. Giant snowflakes whispering around us, confetti clinging to eyelashes. Not love but definitely something close.

* * *

Spring arrives with a week of warm rain and sidewalks blocked by rivers of brown slush. I'm writing exams off the top of my head, picking away at listless essays. Professors can offer no more extensions. 'You're still a *student* here, right?' is how one of them puts it.

For a while now Leah has been spending her days in the library, usually staying in the humid cafeteria for dinners of tortilla chips and machine-made hot chocolate. This routine has become so reliable that I am surprised to come home after my Fascism in Film exam to find her standing in the middle of the living room.

'What's up?'

She says nothing, but bends down to pick up her suitcase. How could I not immediately recognize something as obvious as Leah's giant orange suitcase?

'Separate vacations?' I ask.

'I meant to be gone before you got back. I didn't want this.'

'What's "this"?'

'This fucking sarcastic, self-pitying exchange.'

'Oh. Well, were you at least going to leave me a note?'

'No. I thought it would be clear.'

'Yes. I guess it would've been.'

I back away from the door, give her room to pass. *Don't go,* I say, but only think I say. *I'm still here inside this mask and I can't take it off.*

She lugs the suitcase to the door and moves close enough to me that I can smell how good she smells. I could reach out to her without raising my arm, I could whisper and she'd hear, but nothing happens.

'Just to make this whole scene clear, I'm leaving. You've already chosen the reasons why,' she says without looking. I respond with a nod and another step back.

I watch her go.

Move over to the front window and stand beneath the underwatered spider plant, Leah bumping and spiralling her way down the wonky wrought-iron stairs. *You need her. You're not enough on your own.* I watch her reach the street and head down toward St. Joseph without looking up to see if I'm there. *Don't let this happen.* I think this, knowing I'm wrong, this whole thing is hugely wrong, but nothing happens. *She's not leaving because of your charbroiled face, she's leaving because of you.* I think this. *You are going to be monstrous and alone. You will hate being monstrous and alone.* I think this, too. *You don't believe in anything, not fate or Jesus, but she's the closest thing.*

I think all of these things, but nothing happens.

Sausage Stew

HER SECRET INGREDIENT was blood. Not her own, she said, but what she could talk the butcher at Steinberg's into sluicing into a mason jar for her. She said he told her he really shouldn't be doing this, it's not safe, he could lose his job if anybody got sick. But she smiled and said she was prepared to take the risk and because it was an odd and sexy request he smiled too and filled the jar from what spilled from that day's split pig.

'So I'm not drinking *your* blood?' I ask.

'No. I won't turn you into a vampire,' she laughs, but I find myself checking for teethmarks anyway. You never know. One of the first things she said herself was that this world is full of demons and freaks, and let her eyes rest on me in a way that suggested that she considered herself one or the other.

Her name is Mozambique, but she goes by Moze. Her father is white and her mother is black, both Canadian, although they met in Africa helping out on some famine or other. She tells me this as we walk through the student ghetto towards her place but I'm only half listening, keeping my eyes out for friends who might spot us together. Not that I would be embarrassed to be seen with her, it just wouldn't be perfectly cool if I was. Moze is exactly the sort of girl I never would have met in Toronto before coming to university in another city: raised in Scarborough, closer to poor than rich, public schooled, one-time hippie parents, not white. The co-ed semi-formal mixers my school had with Havergal or Bishop Strachan were populated by girls who would tell elaborate first-person jokes about people like Moze, stories that provided examples of bad taste and ugliness and stupidity. They called them Rocker-Babes or Skanks or Mall Sluts in variously dismissive, nauseated and hateful tones. As for me, I thought they might have been going a little too far sometimes, but some of them were really hot and a lot of it was funny, so usually I didn't say anything.

I'm walking with Moze because she asked me. Just came up at the end of the class we were both in on women writers of the twentieth century and told me she liked my comment about Sylvia Plath and asked if I'd eaten dinner yet.

'No, not yet. And what comment was that?'

'The one about how Plath totally anticipated eating disorders, postmodernism and false memory syndrome.'

'Oh, that. Thanks.'

'I didn't say I *agree* with you. I just liked the way you said it.'

'O.K. And I'll just pretend there's no difference.'

I didn't know her, although I'd noticed her. She was good-looking in the way she worked to hide her good looks: huge sweatshirts covering her slender body, her dark skin blanched by what I took to be a lack of sleep. Nobody seemed to know her and she always walked home alone, almost hidden inside an oversized parka with the hood pulled tight into a funnel around her face.

We walk to her apartment on Durocher, a street level 1 1/2 in a neglected student walk-up. Inside, the front hallway is cluttered with mountain bikes, stacked newspapers and, here and there, discarded or forgotten mail. Some of it, I notice, bears Moze's name. 'Wherever I lay my hat,' she says and unlocks the door with the key that is tied to a strip of leather around her neck.

'Have a seat,' Moze directs unnecessarily, the apartment being so small it immediately produces the feeling that one should sit or lie down so that the space is not entirely taken up by standing bodies. Once seated, we are close enough to the stove and cutlery drawer that Moze doesn't have to get up to serve or pull out spoons. The stew itself contains no easily recognizable flavours, and is made up of an unlikely combination of ingredients (okra, sweet potatoes, chick peas, thumb-sized chunks of pork sausage and, somewhere in there, pig's blood) but it tastes good. My hunger surprises me and I eat without speaking, which is fine because Moze doesn't eat at all but tells stories of her life: an affair with her father's best friend, the same man her mother had been sleeping with since she was seven ('I kept waiting to see what my mother saw'), a time during high school when she left home and supported herself by working a phone sex line, a one-night stand with a guy at Douglas Hall in first year that left him with two shattered knees from jumping out of his window after he called her the next day and she told him to get over it, it was nothing, what did he expect? Commitment?

'I heard about that guy,' I say.

'He said he'd never felt love before me. Can you *believe* that? *Love?* Split parents, alcoholic mom, invisible dad, therapy. Middle-class kid disease. I know I should feel bad. Not responsible, just *bad*. But I don't.'

I tell her it's not her fault, that people have to look out for themselves.

'Dog-eat-dog,' she says.

When I finish eating she clears away the bowls, pouring her uneaten portion back into the pot. Then, without a word, she comes around the table, takes my hand, and pulls me out of the chair and onto the bed. We make out for a while and then she gets up and lights a candle, a tall cylinder of purple wax that, once lit, emits the odour of burnt lavender. Before its fluttering light she undresses in two swift movements and kneels on the bed beside me.

'Let me ask you one thing,' she says. 'Do you get attached to people easily?'

'I think I used to. But I'm trying to cut down.'

She smiles and nods in place of laughing.

The fucking proceeds in quick, rough movements that scrape the futon's wooden frame over the tiled floor. Through it all she shouts praise, challenges and profanities in what I take to be her phone sex voice. Every once in a while she asks, 'You *like* that, don't you?' and when I say yes it's the truth. I've never been with a girl who did these things. My last girlfriend liked to pretend she was her family's maid and I was her father, but that doesn't really count. Moze is *really* into it, poses like a model in some top-rack men's magazine, licking her lips, lifting and squeezing her breasts together with her tiny hands as though a treasured, luxurious burden. Beneath them her ribs show.

Afterwards her body is less sweaty than it is damp, and her

skin turns cool almost instantly. I roll away from her and dry myself on the sheets. Six feet away from the edge of the bed the stew still cooks on the hotplate in a pot too big for the counter. From the floor everything appears even smaller than it did at first. The bathroom has no door and is no bigger than those at the back of buses. The apartment itself is a single room packed with things that don't fit and threaten to come crashing down with one false move: a ceiling-high bookcase, wicker chair, even a bashed around stand-up bass resting on a crooked pile of *Vogues*. There is nowhere to move but on the bed, which lies on the floor as a constant invitation.

In the candle's dim purple light we lie under the open window and listen to passing cars and drunk students heading home from the bars on St. Laurent. 'You're a fucking liar!' a woman's voice shouts clearly into the room from a block away. 'Will you *relax!*' her boyfriend responds. I want to be outside along with them and make my own way home, escape the dampness of the room, the manufactured smell of flowers, the slickness of her skin. I want to call my friends and tell them all about it.

'Do you want to do something?' she asks, back to her normal voice again.

'Sure.'

She lifts herself from the mattress and I can see from the candle and filtered streetlight that she is beautiful, but it's a passing, abstract observation. As she moves out of the light the moment of her beauty dissolves and she becomes only a recognizable shape moving in the dark: a cat loping behind a parked car, an alley raccoon weaving along the top of the backyard fence.

She goes into the bathroom, digs around in the drawer under the sink and comes back with a small tin box, the kind used to keep thread, buttons and pins. Sitting cross-legged on the mattress beside me, she pops the lid open and pulls out a blackened spoon and ball of tin foil. She holds these things in front of me, cocks her head like a quizzical dog.

'Smack, anyone?' she says, pulls out a syringe and lays it between pubic hair and thigh.

'Are you fucking crazy?'

'I'm not telling. I'm asking.'

'That's very scary shit.'

'I figured a private school golden boy like you'd be up for anything.'

I'd never put a needle in my arm. That's what people say, that's what I've said. How do they do it? Of course you know *how*, having seen it done in movies and the hardcore cop shows the American channels broadcast after midnight. The sweaty guy rolling up his sleeve and tying the rubber tube around his arm, pulling it tight with his teeth. Then the close-up of the needle, the expert tapping and little squirt to make sure it's ready and then, closer still, in it goes (always a little hard to watch). Camera pulls back, guy's head rolling on his shoulders and he's letting out a sigh like he's finally made it to a mushy, calm place in his head. That's what it is, that's how it's done. But to actually *do* it. Yourself. For real. It's a hard thing to stick a needle in your arm.

Hard, but not that hard. Moze helps. It's like having a doctor present, her voice urging everything along with the authority of experience mixed with an edge of taunting challenge. 'Yes indeed! Look at those virgin veins!' She strokes the length of my arm until it tingles.

'This is too ...'

'It's just a drug. You raided Daddy's liquor cabinet, and I moved in with a dealer when I was sixteen. The difference is merely cultural.'

'Ha, ha. You go to school on this?'

'I'm gifted. They pay me to be here. It's the Help the One Smart Kid Who Can't Afford It Programme. And the nice thing is, I don't need to make any friends because this is the *cure* for loneliness, golden boy. Not that you'd know anything about *that*.'

While she speaks she taps a vein and keeps her eyes on mine.

'Now. Make a fist. Don't look if you don't want to. Ever given blood? Same thing. Don't tense your muscles up like that, you're not *pumping* up you're *shooting* up. Relax everything but keep your fist. O.K. I'm going to do you now. You'll feel a pin prick, the usual thing, just don't move until I get it out. And then you'll feel a rush: *BOOM!* Something in the stream, kind of sick but not sick, you know? No, you wouldn't know, but you'll see what I mean. O.K. Just chill 'cos I'm ready here ...'

I close my eyes and feel the needle go in. It hurts more than other needles, like it's not in the right place, and I hear Moze say 'Damn!' and play with it a little while it's still in my arm. Then it stops moving and she says *Yes* and lets it go.

Where does it have to go before you feel it – your heart? your brain? Wherever it is, it gets there in the time it takes me to open my eyes. Then all at once I'm sick, I'm hot, I can't breathe, I'm ice, I'm blind. Nothing moves or feels or works.

'How you doin'?' Moze asks from somewhere above me, smiling, not a worry in the world.

'Am I dying?'

'No.'

'I'm going to die.'

'Just relax, man. I'll be with you in a second.'

Then she gets to work on herself. In seconds she's lying beside me, all her energy drained instantly away and eyes glazed with tears, her tongue panting loose in her mouth. We lie still like that together for a while. Maybe a long while. The time passes in regular waves of either nausea or unconsciousness, a black cone being lowered and lifted over my eyes.

'It's like a coma,' I whisper, my mouth caked dry. Beside me, Moze's breathing is fluttery, a rapid series of baby hiccups. When I try to get up I'm exhausted by the effort it takes to raise myself onto my elbow. Below me the bed is speckled with blood. Mine. Most of it has gathered in a line headed by a tiny purple clot and behind it a thin stream passing through the folds in the sheet. In a slow-motion search I check my body for the source and find it beading out from the place where the needle went in. I raise my arm and turn it over but still the blood trails down to my hand, to the end of fingers where it thickens and clings before falling as it did before. Some of it pools in the shallow moat caused by the curve of mattress surrounding Moze's back.

'Hey. Fuck. I'm bleeding.'

She doesn't move or speak. I can't hear her hiccup breathing either.

'Did you have to mess my arm up like this?'

Nothing.

'Don't fuck around. I'm too stoned to deal with a head trip right now, O.K.? Wake up.'

I pull her over onto her back and her head lolls reluctantly with it. There's something wrong: purple lips, a line of sweat under her nose, eyes white as hard-boiled eggs. I put my ear to her chest to listen for her heart but all I hear is my own.

Are you dying? Why die now? Hold on and O.D. tomorrow night, for Christ's sake. What am I supposed to do? Save your life?

I know there are things you can do to bring someone back. There's mouth to mouth (lift back the head, close the nostrils and blow, right?) and heart massage, a pounding above the ribs with open palms. It's all been done on those TV rescue shows, the ones with ten-year-old girls saving the lives of fathers after heart attacks at family picnics. But had any of them just shot up?

This isn't cool. You just blacked out, right? You'll wake up in the morning with a split skull, and you'll call me up and maybe we'll get together for coffee and laugh and say, 'That was some pretty eerie shit last night!' Right?

I decide to leave. Not *decide*, I just do. Somehow I'm thinking clearly enough to pull the sheet up around her chin, close the window and blow out the candle before I go. Drops of my blood end up on the windowsill, the pillow, the bedside table. It looks thinner than blood usually does, a ketchup and water horror-movie mixture. At the door I stop and look back and she melts into the bed, a dusk shadow pulling back into the place it came from.

Out on the street the first thing I want to do is run, head up high into the park on the mountain where nobody goes. Wait to come down, for the burning in my head to cool. Then I think maybe I should call an ambulance. For myself. Don't they have an emergency room antidote for junkies that brings them down? There's a blue glow from a phone booth on the corner that I keep in my sights and levitate towards.

By the time I push the 9 in 9-1-1 my mind changes and I almost turn around but my fingers keep going and hit the two 1's on their own. Somebody should come and clean her up, do whatever needs to be done. But the effort of thinking of someone else for the five seconds it takes for the phone to ring exhausts me. It's stupid that I'm the one who has to do all this.

'*Bon soir. Emergence. Oui!*'

Male, impatient, accusatory.

'There's a girl, three doors up from Milton on the left side of Durocher. She's unconscious. Heroin.'

'o.k. What's her name?'

'Moze.'

'Moses. Last name?'

'I don't know. I've got nothing to do with her.'

'Are you with her now?'

'I left.'

'What's your name?'

'No.'

'Noah?'

'You don't need to know.'

'Are you near the address you gave? Where the girl is?'

'Somebody's dying. I mean, I don't know if she's actually *dying*. She may already be dead. She was cold.'

'Just tell me where you are.'

'I didn't do anything.'

'You left her there alone.'

'I've got nothing to do with her.' I drop the receiver and leave it hanging by its silver snakeskin.

They're going to come. And if they get a hold of me and she's dead they're going to think I had something to do with it, that I was the one who fixed her up. That's manslaughter or something, isn't it, if she's dead? At the very least they'll kick me out of school, which wouldn't be so bad but I like it here, as far as schools go. The old man would have a shit fit. He'd make some speech about how much he'd spent on my education and on 'shaping my character into that of a gentleman' and what little good it had done. And he'd definitely cut the money off and make me move home, which would mean leaving all my friends and giving up my apartment with exposed brick and oak beams and a view of the river.

Best thing is to walk away, it's been one of those nights. Nothing I can do, not really. There's no point in having my name in some cop's notebook just so that they can close the file a little sooner. She fed me that blood stew and then we fucked and shot up but none of that was my idea.

Move, keep moving.

Some day you won't even remember this, golden boy.

Stay away from people. Keep your head down. Don't let them see your face.

Everyone has to live with secrets. This just happens to be your first.

I hunch and scuff east into the sloping, one-way blocks of the Plateau. My eyes stay on the blood that trickles out and down my arm, zags over the lines in my palm to the end of my fingers. Try to go home, but don't remember where it is. Further east, further north, moving in squares and circles. Huddle in corners next to the warmth of restaurant exhaust fans blowing out *souvlaki*, deep-fried Chinese and beer. My body unsure whether to sweat or shiver or throw up or die. The echo of sirens urges me up and further on, past a thousand narrow walk-ups with a thousand Blessed Virgins tiled next to the doors. And all the while the blood is dripping off my fingers, leaving perfect circles on the broken street behind me. It doesn't stop, drips from a hole deep as you think a hole could be. The night slugs on and wraps itself in clouds and the blood still falls, unslowed by healing, from red, red, red, to black and black and black.

House of Mirrors

WHEN I WAS FIVE, and there wasn't much left, my mother took me to the Perth County Fall Fair. There was a petting zoo. For a dollar, a donkey with a slumped spine and flies in its ass carried me around its sawdust pen. A German farmer shouted 'Squeeze!' and pointed at his cow's teats. I warmed a white, hyperventilating chickadee in my hands. A dung-toothed goat licked my face. On the midway (a K-Mart parking lot), there were three rides. They had names like yard-sale paperback mysteries: The Zipper, The Octopus, The House of Mirrors. The last one was a trailer truck full of shiny warped metal that made you fat, thin, multiple, and not there at all. My mother tried to win me a stuffed giraffe by tossing rings at Coke bottles. The man inside the booth looked like Jimmy Durante and spat blue hork in place of laughing. He kept his hand out and said, 'Don't let the little fella down!' My mother's dirt-wrinkled elbow showed through a hole in her sweater, and she kept a cigarette in her mouth as the rings were thrown, bobbled, and rejected. At the end, with the last of the money my father had stuck under the ashtray before he left, she bought me a pair of plastic binoculars. Putting them to my eyes, I looked up at the darkening limestone sky and found the moon, a blue-veined headlight.

'What are you looking at up there? Eh?'

'Nothing.'

'You're not looking at nothing?'

'Nope.'

'Put those down for a second. You can't see nothing 'cause it's dark now, anyway. All the things to see are down here, baby.'

I kept the binoculars set against my eyes and lowered them to the surface of the world. There was a blur of movement and blended colours, a frightening collapse of dimensions, with everything closing in. I pulled the binoculars away and let my mother take me by the hand, a cigarette still scissored in her fingers. The world was clearer now, but it still smelled of straw, pork fat and piss.

She led me off the midway to the crabgrass field behind the Empire Cinema at the far end of the mall where they were going to set off the fireworks. We weaved past the cluttered blankets of chocolate-smeared families to the back where the field was ended by three lines of barbed wire strung low between the thistles. Beyond this was the railway line that ran through town but no longer carried trains since the mill went to half capacity and nothing heavy enough to require a train to carry it was made here any more. That was what my mother told me when I asked her where the tracks led to.

The two men doing the igniting worked hastily, but several black moments still separated each launch. When the rockets finally went off they whistled into the sky and then hung there, caught in the balance of propulsion and gravity, before blowing up in a sulphureous cloud. The colours cast down upon our faces and flashed them into waxy vividness, like the heads of ghouls in children's dreams.

'Whaddya think of that? Eh? Isn't that pretty?'

'Could you see the colours from the moon ... *Mommy?*'

'No. I don't know. We're too small.'

Just then my mother pushed me behind her back when a man I didn't know walked up. He wore boots encrusted with mud and dried asphalt which left marks in the earth where he walked.

'Hey there, Beth! Alone tonight?'

'I'm not alone,' she said, pulled me forward and held my head against her belt buckle. The man looked down at me and lifted one side of his mouth with the muscles in his cheek.

'You've got the little one, do ya? Been playing Mommy all day? Bet you could use a good stiff one.'

The man handed her a small thermos from the inner pocket of his ski jacket and she took a swallow, closed her eyes and took another.

'Easy there, baby!' the man laughed, but did not move to take the thermos away. My mother made a strange sound in her throat, a high giggle, and took a step to stand beside him, resting her head against where his collarbone would be under his plaid work shirt. Lowering his head to her ear he whispered things to her that made her pout, smile, and smack her hand against his chest and shout '*You!*'

Her hands released me and I stumbled away from them, my head craned back to take in the whole of the sky. Another missile exploded directly above and splashed over us all a wriggling umbrella of silver worms.

'Come to me, baby! Oh yeah! Come to me!' a man shouted and made the other men laugh and some of the women too.

When I lowered my head again and looked around me my mother was gone. The man with the boots was gone, too. In that moment, that half-moment, there was a feeling of heavy tar filling my lungs, cutting off the air as it rose. I broke through the circle of people that surrounded the space where we had stood before and then I saw them, standing alone beyond the area of cut grass and almost out of range of the parking lot floodlights. They did not hold each other, but stood close. The man's hands grabbed at her, but fluidly, never lingering in one place for any longer than a single, white-knuckled squeeze. My mother didn't move away, but did not touch him back. As in one of those old photos of marathon dance contests she stood slack-kneed in his arms, ready to fall if he broke apart from her. Above, the sky flashed blue with burning tinsel.

I ran, head down, watching my feet move in a cartoon blur. I ran until the tar in my chest reached the top of my throat and forced me to stop.

'Lost your Mommy, honey?' a fat man asked me. I was crying, but soundlessly. He was close enough to my face for me to smell his sour-butter sweat and for him to see my silent tears in the dark.

'No.'

'Let's take a look for her. Hey? Take my hand.'

He was so fat he looked sick before he looked fat. His fatness appeared as a terrible swelling over his entire body that blackened the skin under his eyes and puffed his fingers into red sausages.

'I'll be your buddy. Go for a walk with me. Hey? Find your Mommy?'

'No!'

I ran from him and he followed until his fatness closed off his lungs and I turned to see him planted still, hands on knees, his mouth open and dumb. Still he raised his hand to me, waving me back, so I moved into the shadows of the Home Crafts tent until he gave up and rolled his body back into the field.

I circled back, followed the railway track and looked for my mother, who was not in the place she was before. Between explosions the sky was darker than a night without a moon, although the moon was out, a blood orange stuck in the branches of a dead maple. The other children in the field, who seemed only seconds ago to have been squealing and sobbing at the booms and sparkles in the sky were now gone, leaving only hushed adults, half standing and half sitting, with nowhere to go until the last missile was sent up.

I walked toward the lights of the midway, believing that my mother had been given money by the man with the boots and was trying again to win at the ring toss. In the wash of pale floodlight, men in loose jeans walked ahead of women in grease-stained pyjama bottoms, the flesh of their legs swollen inside their skin, their hands stuck to the syrupy hands of waddling, child-sized versions of themselves. They did not speak to each other, but sometimes the child would wail for more candy floss or root beer and the man would look at the woman and the woman would tell the child to shut the hell up right now or clip the back of its head with her palm.

Every time the Zipper went up there was the sound of girls screaming inside the spinning cages and boys laughing 'H-o-l-y s-h-i-t!' beside them as the change fell out of their pockets and clanged off the rusty struts to the ground. The man who operated the machine smoked with one hand and kept his other on the control knob. When someone inside the cages begged 'Stop this thing!' or started throwing up or bawling from fear, it was his job not to turn or look up.

People looked at me only if I stood in their way. The men who worked the stalls were unhooking the giant stuffed giraffes and parrots from over their heads and throwing them into piles in the corner while long-lit cigarettes bounced and stiffened in their mouths. The ring toss man smiled at me as I passed but did not stop spitting gobs over the counter into the sleeping black cables and caramelized garbage that covered the painted lines of the parking lot. My mother was not there, or at any other game, though I walked the midway until they shut down the generators and the coloured bulbs turned brown in their sockets.

I started to run. Away from the smell of sugar and dumpsters and into the darkness of the back field. But before I could reach the place where the other people were an old man wearing shit-caked jeans grabbed my ankle. He lay in a patch of prickly weeds so high he was invisible unless you stood directly over him. When he raised his head and rolled closer a smell of grain alcohol and slaughtered animal rose up from his skin.

'Bugger almost stepped on my face,' he said to nobody but himself, his eyes level with my knees. Then he drank enough rye in one go to make his adam's apple bob three times in his neck.

'They can take what they want. Have it, ya bitches, it's yours. But you can't take what I got. No sir, that's mine.'

I didn't know if he was talking about me, my ankle, or something else entirely, whatever had put him there in weeds that left cuts he couldn't feel across his cheeks. Then, without changing his face, he peeled his fingers back from my skin and descended again into the depression his body had made in the earth and was gone.

Too tired now, I walked through the field to the ball diamond where they let people park their cars. I found our station wagon, green with a plastic side panel made to look like wood. There was no one inside, but I pressed my face against the driver's side window and searched the interior with my eyes as though she could be hiding in the shadows under the seats. Eventually I let my knees buckle and sat with my back against the door, let the mud moisten and creep into my pants. I didn't think I had closed my eyes until they popped open to the sound of the man with the boots shouting, 'Wakey-wakey there, fella!'

The two of them stood over me, a few feet away, my mother clasped in front of him but held close. He thought I couldn't see his hand hooking up the back of her skirt, or didn't care if I could. My mother kept her pupils fixed on a point somewhere above my head and forced out whinnies of laughter.

'Good boy! You found the car! I knew you weren't lost,' she said, and laughed.

'How you doin' there, pal?' the man said, and moved his free hand underneath her sweater, grabbing her breast as though it were the head of a fish.

'*Don't!*' my mother yelped.

'Don't what?'

'Not *here.*'

'Where?'

'You're *awful!*'

But she did nothing to free herself from his hands. Instead she took in a wheezy breath, tried to laugh again, caught something in her throat, and started to cough with her tongue half stuck out her mouth. The man released her enough so that she could double over and spit in the boot-scarred mud.

'Get in the car,' she said to me when she had straightened. Her eyes were instantly bloodshot.

'Where you goin'?' the man asked, and faked a pout.

'Time to call it a night.'

'I don't think so.'

Then he bit my mother's neck. Or he tried to, but she swung away from him, and suddenly his hands were free, and he didn't know where to put them. They twitched at his sides like snakes tied up by their tails.

'Slut. Aren't you gonna suck me off?' There was anger in his voice, but also real dismay, a boyish confusion.

'Get in the car,' my mother said to me, lifted me up by my arm, and threw me in on the driver's side.

'Your mom there's known as a right good cocksucker! Did you know that, little friend?' the man shouted at me, his lips pulled back from too-small teeth. 'She'll *blow* and she'll *blow* and she'll *BLOW* your balls off!'

My mother is beside me turning the ignition and rolling up the window at once. Without looking my way her arm lashes out and presses against my chest, hard but briefly, as though to make sure I'm there.

'Another time then?' the man laughed too loudly, his busy hands now turned into fists pounding down on the car's roof. 'I'll just have to take a raincheck, won't I, little sister? Yeah, we'll get together later, and you know it's true!'

* * *

We smudged out of town, the station wagon lolling at every curve on exhausted suspension. My mother rolled down her window and let in the sound of tires breathing over warm pavement. The air that entered was damp, and carried the caky-sweet smell from the plant mixed with roadkill skunk.

We took the concession road east to where our house was. There were no lights on except for a flash of blue television light from the front room, but I knew it didn't mean that my father was home because it was always on, with the volume turned down to almost nothing but loud enough to speak to me at night and lull me to sleep with bursts of studio audience laughter.

She drove past the two cement horse heads at the end of the gravel lane without slowing down. Didn't turn her head, didn't speak, breathed steadily though the narrow corner of her mouth so that the tip of her cigarette glowed orange every few seconds like a railway warning signal.

'We're going for a drive,' my mother whispered, more to herself than to me. The green dashboard light turned the shadows on her face into comic-book exaggerations. 'That's what we're gonna do. Just go for a drive.' She lit a cigarette, cried and laughed and spat and put her hand on my leg and blew smoke out her nose. For the moments she closed her eyes I kept my own eyes open and stared straight down the road, imagining that she could see where she was going through me so long as I sat still and didn't blink.

At the corner of the headlights' beam animal eyes flashed out from the dark trees. I ached to turn around to see if they would come along with us, urge us to pull over so they could guide us into the woods where they could teach us to survive in the wild. But I did not turn or move, kept my eyes on the highway's centre yellow lines as they were one by one swallowed up under the car's blunt hood. I did not turn or move, knowing that without the light in their faces the animals were invisible at night, and that they liked it that way. I did not turn or move, already certain that nothing in the living world would ever do anything for us but turn its head just long enough to watch us pass.

The Earliest Memory Exercise

MY GROUP HAS started something new. It works just the way you'd expect it to. Think back to the very first thing you remember in your life, it could be anything. It doesn't have to make any kind of sense, you don't have to know the people in it. The memory may be as insignificant as a fallen pine cone, a spanking, dropping stewed yams on your head, a yellow balloon set adrift. As long as it's the first is good enough for the doctor.

'Close your eyes. Take your time. Go back step by step, find the place where you can't go back any further,' he says with practised sympathy in his voice, as though we are about to experience a severe but necessary physical pain, a spinal tap or rectal.

'I've got mine!' says Morris after about five seconds. If this were the sort of thing where you were given grades, Morris would be the keener of the class.

'What do you remember, Morris?'

'Peanut butter,' he says, opening his eyes and sighing. 'I'm spreading peanut butter over my legs with a kitchen knife.'

Morris offers his self-interpretation to the group before anyone has a chance to think. We are the audience to his banalities. He shares every revelation with enthusiasm, in a plaintive 'Don't you *see*?' tone.

'The peanut butter must be paint. It denotes my creativity. As I've told you all before, I love to paint. It's an artistic *drive*.'

'Wait a second, Morris,' I say. 'It might be feces.'

The doctor scowls in my direction, taps his expensive fountain pen against his lip.

'What?' says Morris, looking around at the rest of the group as if they are his most loyal friends, ready for the signal to attack.

'Shit. The first thing you remember is spreading it down your legs, and you've been spreading it around ever since.'

Morris gapes, reddens, slumps.

'We've talked about open communication before. Do we need to discuss it again?' the doctor says, turning to me.

'No.'

'Good. I think we'd all prefer *channels* to *fences*. Now, I'm sorry, Sylvia. You're next.'

* * *

We've been told that the purpose of the exercise is twofold. First, it puts you in touch with the distance between your present self and who you once were. It achieves *temporal awareness*.

The second function it serves involves what the doctor calls *rediscovery*. The thinking is that whatever the nature of your first memory, it foreshadows the character of your present psychological state. In some central, symbolic way, what we recall at the origins of ourselves defines us for the rest of our lives.

'We're searching for the initial emotional landmark,' says the doctor, looking around at us with his eyebrows bound up in painful concentration.

I watch Morris fume and implode in the corner, but I know it doesn't take long for him to recover. Still, there is a vague but real tingle of guilt in watching him. I'm not sure why I'm like this, but I can't help it. When I hear his voice something rises in me that's cruel and dismissive and bullying, and it refuses to be calmed. It's something in his face, I think. The coil of fat under his chin. Or the ass-waving way he walks. Or, like I said, maybe it's something in his voice.

During the bathroom break (the doctor calls it 'intermission') I apologize, and Morris accepts with his head hanging from his neck like a rib-kicked dog.

'Why do you say those things?' he asks without looking up.

'I don't know.'

'I mean, in front of the others –'

'I don't know, Morris.'

'You must have been a victim yourself, sometime. Now you torment others to get even with your past. The doctor said that might explain it.'

'Yes. I'm sure you're both right.'

'Do you want to know something? And I say this for your own good. You can't move forward unless you open up, rule number one. I think you've got something you need to work out, and you haven't even started on it yet.'

'Thanks, Morris. I'll get to work right away.'

'God!' Morris spits. 'Have you *always* been this way?'

I shrug. The truth is, I think I've always enjoyed pointing out the smallness of other people's problems. It's not that mine are any bigger, but they're mine, and I get along fine with them. I'm only here because they're making me go as part of the conditions of my release. I won't go into that, if you don't mind, aside from saying that you'd be surprised how willing some people are to believe the first sob story they hear from a mean, messed-up sonofabitch.

There are things that are meant to be told, and others kept private. This view makes me totally wrong for therapy, I know. Too *unyielding*, to use the doctor's term. This is because I believe that secrets aren't keys to some mind puzzle, a Chinese box that must be opened by an intricate code in order to be understood. Secrets, as anybody whose ever done the kind of shit I've done knows, are nothing more or less than modest and sensible ways of managing our lives.

* * *

We work our way around the circle. One by one, everyone shares their first memory with the others, sketching out the foggy details with bowed, struggling faces. It's the difficulty of recollection itself, of calling things up from the corners that seems to defeat them, not the wound of whatever the particular memory holds. After a short while their words melt together, I drift in and out. They lose me in the long, stagy pauses with their eyes rolled up to the ceiling for answers. They seem to all be asking God if they're getting it right and, if not, for Him to just send down some words for them to say. When they finish they look to the doctor for approval, who offers them his engrossed nods without exception.

One member tells a story about sitting in a treehouse and watching her father have a heart attack as he mowed the front lawn. There was a terrible guilt that came out of this episode because she didn't climb down or call for help, only sat up in the tree and watched him writhe on the lush suburban grass. She provides details which include a barking dog, sky the colour of worn denim, white foam running from the corners of her father's mouth. While the story stopped the group cold for a while, the doctor gently disqualified it by pointing out that we should try to find the earliest, not necessarily the most traumatic memory of our past.

'Go back beyond childhood,' he encouraged the rest of us, his hands in a pushing gesture. 'There is so much *formation* before the age of three.'

But as far as interesting stories go, the doctor has pushed us back too far. Now all we're getting are vomitings, falls down stairs, broken toys, hot breath from hairy adult faces. Without being asked, Morris cuts in to add something about riding a donkey at his uncle's farm. 'His back was permanently arched from being ridden all the time by us kids. He had yellow teeth and smelled like wet hay. And he was so *dusty*.'

I've got some time because I'm last in the circle, although I don't need it. I know what my earliest memory is already.

I remember being in a crib, lying on my stomach with the side of my face settled in a white cotton pillow. My mother and father are on vacation, and we have taken a long drive to a hotel. It's near sea water: I can smell the unfamiliar salt in the air, and there is the fuzzy, far-off sound of the tide. Years later, clearing things out of the drawers of my father's apartment, I found a leather photo album. It was full of black-and-white pictures with captions at the bottom penned in his jagged hand. There was one picture that told where we were. It's of me wrapped in a tartan blanket being held by my father on the front steps of the hotel, his face surly and thin-lipped. My right hand is reaching out to the camera and my mouth is a perfect oval, crying for my mother. Under the photo my father had written *Celtic Lodge, Nova Scotia*. Below this there is a reference to my age at the time, the only information my father made sure the album consistently provided: *Tom. Nineteen Months*.

But this is all secondary. It doesn't count.

What I truly remember is watching my parents through the

painted white prison bars of my crib. They are in the middle of a fierce argument, pacing between the bedroom and cramped, fluorescent bathroom. The space is too small for them to move around in this way, but when they bump into each other they don't seem to notice. It's like they're wind-up soldiers, mindless but alive, moving dutifully along determined paths. When they aren't moving they stand apart and trade cruelties, one after the other but never overlapping, both allowing the other time to come up with new and more calculated abuse. Their faces are lowered, red, inflated. I remember how all of this anger is at the same time restrained, they're not letting go like they would if they were at home. They must keep it under control or the hotel manager will interrupt them, perhaps order them to leave.

My mother is young. I know this for a fact, of course. But in my memory she looks her age. Twenty-one. She is threatening to leave us forever. You won't believe this, but I knew this was what it was about at the time, listening from the lilac-scented blankets of my rented foldaway crib. I know this as well as my own hunger or the lemon-peel smell of my mother's skin.

In this argument my mother is more controlled than my father, relentless, finishing each of her sentences despite his attempts at interruption. *Stop it! Stop it!* he shakes pitifully, but spits out *Thankless bitch* the moment she finishes her thought. He wears his injury like a heavy blanket that rounds his shoulders and bends his back. A ruined giant, a Goliath. But every few minutes his self-pity flares into rage, and his hand slams down on the flimsy night table next to the bed. Once his watch, which he has taken off and left on the varnished wood surface (and today sits in a velvet Crown Royal bag among my socks) falls to the floor.

But here's the part of my earliest memory that would send the doctor into a note-taking spasm: My father is sitting on the edge of the bed with his back to me, sobbing into his hands. My mother stands outside the bathroom door with her arms crossed over her sunken chest. She has thrown her wedding ring into the corner (a dramatic, conclusive gesture borrowed from a movie). She is crying, too, but with resolution. After a minute of building and evening her breath, she says to my father while looking directly into my eyes, 'If it weren't for *him* I'd leave you right now.'

My father raises his heavy, mastiff's head and turns it toward me, his face cut with tears. He speaks to my mother although his eyes look into me alone and do not turn away.

'Then go, for Christ's sake. Go. I can do this on my own. Go. Just don't ever come back if you do,' he says, his voice lowering to a whisper. 'You never wanted him in the first place.'

That's the end of it. My mother does not argue. She doesn't disagree.

* * *

My first memory is ready. The guy before me finishes telling of how his favourite sweater was lost by being buried in the sand at Lake Huron by his brother whom he's hated ever since.

The doctor settles his saggy eyes upon me: 'And you?'

'Marbles,' I say.

The group nods. Morris lowers his head as if he knew this all along.

'I'm looking into a bag of shiny glass I believe are priceless jewels.'

There's a moment of respectful silence while everyone pretends to consider this. Morris pendulums his shoes over the brown carpet in satisfaction, squaring his conclusions away. The doctor scribbles a brief note, straightens his posture for his little end-of-the-session announcement.

'Okay. I think that was very illuminating for all of us. Perhaps now we should take a deep breath and think to ourselves about what all of this means.'

Then he closes his eyes and the rest of us do the same, as though joining him in a silent prayer.

Camp Sacred Heart

IT WAS ACTUALLY called that. Those words were arched over the gravel road entrance in a sign made of nailed-together logs of knotty birch. But a voice from the back of the bus reads it differently. 'Camp Smelly Fart!' it shrieks.

I'm bouncing around on the green vinyl school bus seat, thinking about *homesick*. That's the word my father used when he saw me off at the Immaculate Conception parking lot. 'Don't get homesick,' he said sharply, more as a command than a compassionate warning. He made it sound like another of the bothersome things he didn't want, as a father, to be obliged to deal with.

It must have been the first time I'd thought about the word, because it sounded strange. It didn't occur to me that the word meant missing home, a desire to go back. Why would I ever miss the silent, curtained home that my father and I shared? But there it was anyway, an aching heaviness in my stomach, a tightness in my throat. It was more than missing, it really was like being sick. But I know it isn't my father I miss.

The bus moves through the woods, pine branches slapping and scratching the windows as we bump inside. Sunlight breaks through the trees to the dark ground in murky shafts, as if passing through narrow church windows.

'Hey! Bus driver! Speed up a little bit, speed up a little bit, speed up a little bit...!' the back-of-the-bus-boys sing.

* * *

The Captain is there to meet us when the bus parks in front of the wooden cross made of tied-together canoe paddles at the foot of the steps up to the lodge. He owns the camp and lives on the grounds, in a shabby cottage surrounded by sickly firs at the edge of the lake. He is red-faced, wears a felt sailor's cap, has a bloated nose and walks with a heavy, wincing limp. For these reasons Captain is the best name anyone can give him. It's so good he calls himself by it.

'Hulloo! Hulloo! Welcome back, boys! This is your Captain speaking!' he calls as we clamber off the bus.

'Hey! Captain!' some of the older boys yell back. By their half-hidden laughter and shared smirks I can tell they know how seriously to take him. But he frightens me slightly, nevertheless. I think it is his lurching, almost monstrous movements. Or maybe the way he speaks about God all the time.

'God bless all of you!' he shouts, squeezing the shoulders of some of the boys he recognizes. 'Praise be to God!'

From behind me a voice says *'Bless this mess!'* in an exaggerated version of the Captain's enthusiastic tone. When I turn I face a boy maybe a year or two older than I am. He has, even at that age, a face shaped by what looks like suffering: lips downturned at the corners, darkly bruised eyes, skin dotted with pale freckles. He is beautiful though, and I even think that at the time. I think the word *beautiful* when I look at him although, being a boy, I know that it isn't supposed to fit.

'Bible freaks scare me,' he says, and smiles. It is a bold thing to say to someone you don't know on the first day at a church camp.

'They scare me, too,' I say. This seems to please him, and he extends his hand in an adult way. When I shake it I feel the bones in his fingers as fine and pronounced, but strong too.

'My name's Laurence,' he says.

'I'm David.'

'Good to meet you, David.' He slings his duffel bag over his shoulder, and I notice a garlanded crest on it, a famous downtown private school. My father called private school boys and the parents that sent them there *snots*, a word that conjured images of greenish goo and gaping nostrils. Laurence's nose is clean and rather small, with a tight bridge of freckles passing over it.

'Let me show you your cabin. We're in the same one together, I think. Unless there's another David here.'

We check with the Captain. No, I am the David.

'David's a biblical name. Did you know that?' the Captain asks me, checking his clipboard list.

I tell him yes, that I have been told that before. He smiles, apparently satisfied with this answer, and hobbles off to shout at and organize the other boys.

'Come right this way,' Laurence says to me, and starts off across the small playing field toward the trees where the cabins are. I grab my own bag and follow him, wondering what I should do next to impress or amuse, what it takes to make a friend.

* * *

I didn't do anything special, but Laurence and I turn out to be friends anyway. Quickly, the two of us become well known as a team, and the others can tell that it is the sort of thing that is difficult to become a part of. Laurence knows his way around the place (this was his third summer) and he knows most of the other boys. They all like him, but at the same time he manages to keep them all at whatever length he chooses. We enjoy the privileges of a sophisticated social power: nobody wants to be the ones we talk about.

It is a private friendship, based on inside jokes and code words. We huddle together on the fringe of things. While the other boys perform physical, occasionally cruel stunts upon each other (which they call practical jokes if confronted by a counsellor, as in, 'It was *only* a practical joke!') Laurence and I make up TV shows and comedy routines. In these little skits it's always madness taking over something, insanity infiltrating a serious and sober scene. A lunatic somehow breaks onto the set of a news broadcast and reads his own items written in crayon. A compulsive, gleeful farter sits in the front pew while the priest continues with mass. All along, I never oppose Laurence's assumption that he play the lunatic or priest. He was the one who could say the words in the right way.

Laurence and I have our own world together. But it is a world designed by him, he gives it shape and definition, all surveyed from a superior and sarcastic vantage point. He makes me laugh at things I never thought were funny, or ever could be. I can listen to him make jokes about the Captain, other boys, his parents or my father (who I told him about) until they are all reduced to ridiculous cartoons. He makes it seem like this is what they all deserve.

* * *

Laurence tells me the story of how the Captain lost his wife. The funny thing is, the version he tells involves a *losing* of her, an actual misplacement. They went out for a walk in the woods behind the dining hall one night, and he stepped away from her for a moment to take a piss or something, and when he came back she was gone. He called for her, he prayed, he called the Gravenhurst cops. She was gone, though. Lost.

This is not the version the Captain himself tells me in his cottage the afternoon I stepped on a rusty nail on the dock and had to have my foot bandaged. I sit on his bed, which is narrow and lumpy like the ones we sleep on in our mildewy cabins, while my bare leg is taken up by the Captain's hands. He studies my wound carefully with screwed-up eyes as if the bottom of my foot is covered with small, unfamiliar print. 'It's not so bad,' he says, raising his head to look at me down the length of my outstretched leg. 'We'll just put a little something on it.'

He moves loudly around his tiny room, searching for scissors and antiseptic and medical tape. As he wraps the cotton over my foot he speaks without looking up, his voice suggestive of forces and authorities that are beyond us, deserving of reverence. Every sentence is separated by a pause, as if he needs time to rest or think.

'This is where my wife died,' he says. Where? The bed? I raise my hands from the blanket and tuck them under my arms.

'She was good to me. But toward the end she was a great burden, ill for so long. That was the worst part: being alive and not being *alive*. And *me*, her husband, caring for her like a child.'

He says this as though it was his caring and not her dying that troubled him. Everything he says has this unexpected doubleness about it, a second meaning that couldn't have been intended. He sighs and I feel his breath pass over the sunbleached hairs of my leg and hear the air catch in his lungs. Even from where he sits I can smell his air as yeasty and rotten but also vaguely perfumed.

'But everybody dies, David,' he says. 'You've got to live

while you're here, it's a blessing. Do what you like, what feels good. Fill your life with pleasure.'

Pleasure. Not a religious word. He keeps spinning the bandage over my foot and pulling on his breath. His voice and the slow circling motion of his arm make me sleepy, but I fight to keep my back straight. This is not the place to be relaxed.

'Thank you, sir,' I say. I keep my eye on the door.

'It doesn't matter what you have to do to be happy,' he whispers, raising his eyes and looking up at me as if my toes were a rifle sight. The top half of his head looks startlingly like my father's: severely creased forehead and disapproving brows. 'God wants us to be happy. He doesn't care about rules, really. That's not what He's about. God *forgives*.'

For a moment he stares and I feel expected to say something. If I knew what he was talking about maybe I would have, but instead I sit silently. Outside, campers are playing soccer and kick the ball against the wall of the cottage, and it thumps somewhere above my head and rattles the plates in the cupboard. This sound seems to retrieve the Captain from another place, because he stops staring, puts down my leg and stands up, moves for the door and holds it open.

'You'll be *just fine*,' he says as I move out down his steps, and again I hear the dual meaning of his tone. Is it my foot that will be fine? Or is it me as a whole, something more essential that is not right but can still be fixed?

* * *

Every morning, as long as it isn't raining, we all assemble for prayers at the Chapel in the Trees. The Captain himself had given it this name, and whenever he repeats it, it is as if a momentary mist passes over his eyes.

'We are gathered here today,' he starts, standing behind his lectern which is a high tree stump, 'to praise God in the midst of His nature, here in the most beautiful of natural churches, the Chapel in the Trees.'

After this there are some prayers that we all have to repeat while standing up, reading the lines from ratty hymn books kept in a milk crate. Then the Captain gives a sermon, which always has a solid, parable-like title. *The Samaritan Camper.*

The Swimmer and the Sinner. The sermons are his own, written on folded lined paper which he keeps in the breast pocket of his rumpled safari shirt. The stories are usually interesting enough, involving people who don't listen to their elders and go on to learn hard lessons.

I can't tell Laurence I like the Captain's stories, however, because he has already decided to target them. When he whispers scornful remarks to me during chapel I have to laugh, despite my feelings for the old man. I look up and see the Captain working his way through his own writing, my head half-turned at the same time to hear Laurence whisper about his cap, his dated and naïve word choices ('Dick was very embarrassed, knowing he had made a real boner'), his hands hanging on to the tree stump to hold himself up. The terrible, giddy thing about it comes from looking at our victim while we dissect him. My laughter is impossible to restrain precisely because of the guilt I feel in directing it at the Captain right in front of his pink, pious face.

* * *

For the boys of the camp the Rock is the dark temple that stands in a kind of mystical opposition to the safe and fragrant Chapel in the Trees. It's regarded as mysterious, otherworldly, possibly haunted. This reputation is furnished by stories, which are privately told in the cabins or in the whispered corners of the campfire. These have to do with the usual occult myths: vengeful spirits, decapitations, Indian burial grounds. The Captain's wife lived there now, a witch ready to prey upon lost or curious campers. Everyone knows these are fictions because there are so many versions that they cancel each other out. Still, there is something that lingered about the Rock, as if all these stories collectively made up a trace of their own truth.

The Rock itself is the jutting, stone-bared face of a small cliff in the woods, about a quarter of a mile behind the cabins. Remembering it now, I know it must have been only about twenty feet high, but it seemed hostile and impassable to me then. This was probably because of Laurence's story about the boy who died trying to climb it.

'He said he wasn't scared, it was only a rock. He told everyone that he was going to climb it on his own. Nobody believed him. But one night he went out there, yelling "You're all chickenshits! There's nothing out there in the woods!" as he left. The next morning, he wasn't in his bunk. When the counsellors went to look for him they found him at the bottom of the Rock, his legs and arms twisted up like a broken doll.'

'Really?'

'Yes. They weren't sure what had done it; the Rock, an animal, or some *thing*.'

'Like what?'

'Who knows? Anything you like. Make up your own nightmare.'

Laurence laughs, and his face is squared by his open mouth. He loves to laugh this way, but he does so rarely around anyone but me.

'You mean it never happened?'

'I mean it *might* have happened.'

It strikes me now that this was enough for me then, the mere possibility of the incredible. It was enough for me that Laurence, on the last night of the month, suggested we go out to the Rock for ourselves. He didn't exactly suggest it either, it was one of his *ideas*.

'Let's go to the Rock tonight,' he says in our cabin when the others are out playing baseball on the athletics field below. I can hear their shouts and name-calling through the thin, warped pine walls. The smells of barbecued meat drift up from the puffing chimney of the dining hall. 'We can talk there,' he says.

So after dinner that night, after grace, black hamburgers and the post-dessert prayer with its recurrent theme of excessive gratitude for the many good things in life, Laurence heads back to the cabin to grab the flashlight and then into the woods with me trailing behind him. This is the usual formation: Laurence ahead and me behind, catching whatever it is he says as it drifts over his shoulder like the wake left behind a water-cutting ship. It is difficult to see or notice anything else. There is the night, our movement, his voice. The flicking sounds of the leaves and sticks being kicked up by our feet. Ahead, the flashlight's beam jumping from the path to the spindly branches above that cut us off from moonlight or stars.

When we reach the Rock I can't see it, but Laurence spots it, stopping in his tracks and whispering in a parody of adventure-movie awe, *'There she is.'*

'Where?'

He moves aside and circles the flashlight over the vine-covered rock face.

'C'mon,' Laurence says after a moment of thought. His flashlight plays around the boulders at the bottom, searching for a path. 'We can go up this way. We can hide.'

The first rocks come up to my waist, and Laurence has to help me up. Once we reach the main body of the cliff the going is slow, for reasons other than the darkness. There is little to grab hold of; the few roots and grasses growing out of the cracks pull away easily in our hands. It makes me think of pulling hair out of a dead man's head. A dim, turfy sound and it's gone.

'Don't fall and die,' Laurence says, laughing over his shoulder above me.

'Thanks a lot.'

'If you go, I go. The Captain will throw me in the lake with cement blocks tied to my toes if he found out I was responsible for the death of a junior camper.'

'God bless him.'

'God bless *you*, my boy! Christ keep *you*!'

'Where are we going?'

'A secret place.'

'So secret even you don't know where it is.'

'All friends must have secrets between them. That's the rule. And now that we know each other so well, it's time that we make one up.'

Laurence has made it to a kind of plateau, a ledge six feet long and broad enough to sit on with your legs hanging partially over the edge and your back against the rock. We get settled beside each other, breathing deeply from the climb, and look into the woods made of trees we cannot see.

'Do you trust me?' Laurence asks after a moment, once our

eyes have gotten used to the dark and we can see as far as the other's face.

'Yes.'

'Would you like to have a secret between us? Do you want to do something secret?'

'Sure.'

'Okay. Promise? Just you and me?'

'Yeah. Promise.'

Laurence places his hands on my knees, slides them up my thighs. He is not afraid, his eyes look directly into mine and show only a wide, concentrated excitement. One hand stops at where my shorts meet my leg, the other reaches up to my waist and undoes the top button. It grasps the tag of my zipper, works its way down. 'Yes,' he whispers.

There is no hesitation. Every movement is deliberate, steady and precise. A moment ago we were breathing heavily from the climb, and as his hand slides inside my shorts we hold our air tightly in our lungs.

'No,' I say, moving my legs up against my chest. My voice seems to come from somewhere else. 'Thank you. No.'

Immediately I am ashamed. I said 'thank you' as if he were offering me candy or a cigarette, some minor indulgence that children are warned against. The shame comes also from betraying him: I had never before stopped him in anything he wanted or said. For this his face falls a little, confused. It indicates disappointment or injury, but I can't tell how sincere it is. He's good at this sort of thing, the representation of feeling.

'Don't you want me?' he asks.

'What do you mean?'

'Do you like me?'

'Yes.'

'Then why don't you touch me?'

'I don't know.'

'Don't you want me? Let me hold you.'

'I don't know.'

'Let me. Yes? Please?'

'I don't think so.'

'Please? Touch me.'

His face is a combination of intent pleading and, just below it, an almost grave aggression. It is the face of desire that depends upon permission but would do anything to achieve it, to hear the final release of the *Yes*. His hands work their way again up my legs, and they stroke a warm circle under my shorts, where the skin is uncoloured by the sun.

'Don't go,' he says. 'Please don't go.'

'I'm not going anywhere.'

He leans over and I feel his face in front of mine, a circle of warmth in the dark, and then lips, pressing hard. I let him. He opens his mouth and at the same time opens mine. For a moment I reach for him, or at least believe I am about to, to encircle his neck in my arms. My hands lift from the rock we sit on, but they do not raise themselves enough. It's like reaching out for mountains while looking at them through the wrong end of binoculars. When he pulls back from me his words still come from very close.

'Don't go, David. Don't leave me. Love me.'

'Yes,' I say, slowly bringing my legs up again against my chest. His hands move away once more, but they wait by his sides.

'Just love me.'

'Yes.'

But there is no loving after that. There is only an adjusting and buttoning of clothes, a shifting space between us, and a long silence, thick with crickets.

* * *

The next morning is Saturday, the end of the month and the last day of camp. I wake up to find that Laurence has already packed his bag and left his bunk. Looking around, I see that the other boys in the cabin are gone too, and the sound of coughing buses from across the playing field tell me I'm late.

I run down to the gravel road where the buses rumble next to each other, surrounded by boys shouting for no reason, worked up for the ride home. I start to look for Laurence but the Captain suddenly comes up before me and I can't move around him. I didn't see where he came from but there he is, blocking my way, his mud-covered Wellingtons a foot away from my sneakers. He is speaking to me, in a voice entirely unlike the authoritative tone he used for the sermons in the Chapel in the Trees. Now it is soft, fatherly, permissive.

'Don't worry, David,' the Captain bends and says in my ear. 'You never really lose your friends. You never really lose anyone.' I realize that this is the closest I have been to him, an opportunity to look at his red and whiskery face. Close enough to see that his lips are cracked, that he has tiny red veins networked through his nose.

'But then, I know you'll be all right,' he goes on. 'You have courage.'

I work up a half-smile, having no idea what he meant. Then a shock of fear bolts up my spine: Did he know about Laurence? The Captain places his hand on my shoulder. His touch is firm and oddly necessary, as if I would topple over or disintegrate altogether if he weren't keeping me in place.

'I mean your name: David. You really should read the Bible,' he says, but mildly, without consternation. 'David and Goliath.'

'Yes,' I say although I don't know the story, only recognize the names.

'A boy called David,' he says mistily, squeezing my shoulder with his thick-knuckled hand. 'You'll see,' he nods with certainty before turning around. 'Read the Bible. It's full of stories.'

Then his back is to me and he's limping away, his cap tilted on his head and his body sloped over itself, lowering into the ground.

* * *

I turn and look for Laurence. He is on a different bus; his goes to Forest Hill, mine to the Scarborough suburbs. When I eventually spot him he is standing behind his bus talking with other boys I had never met. I smile and come closer, but he does not smile back, just watches me while he talks. He doesn't stop, goes right on with his story, a joke about the Captain's bad leg.

On the bus I find a seat on my own at the back, position myself next to the window. I keep looking for Laurence as the bus roars and jolts its way out of the narrow lane. My eyes stay at the window as the bus moves into the woods, reaches the highway and turns back towards the city. I keep looking long after the trees give way to farmers' fields, billboards and, eventually, the rows and rows of housing developments and mall parking lots. I look for him in the place where my father picks me up, throws my bag in the trunk and drives me home without asking how it was, what I did or if it was any fun.

Sometimes I look even now, on the streets of the city where I live. Laurence doesn't haunt my life, yet he never leaves me entirely alone. In the black moments before sleep, in the hypnotized states of travel, work or boredom, he often comes and joins me. In these daydreams there's not much that he does; there is only his smile, the being-next-to-me, his slender beauty.

It's not me that he wants, exactly. And it's not guilt I feel when I think of him. It isn't shame, regret, love, forgiveness, or desire. But that's all part of it, too.

Breaking and Entering

I am walking through a field with my father. The sky is lowering and black above us, dense clouds squeezing together like swollen intestines. Ahead of us is an irrigation ditch, a cornfield and beyond it a red brick farmhouse with a single light on in its kitchen. There is a feeling, a knowledge that if we reach the house we'll be safe, but it is impossibly far away and beside me my father moves ploddingly, can't raise his feet, stumbles over the mounded grass in his untied black Oxfords.

A twisting funnel descends from the clouds, a black tube settling upon a neighbouring field, exploding earth, rocks and roots up around it. The sound it makes is the scream of tires before the crash. I take my father's arm over my shoulder and lead him toward the farmhouse, knowing we will not make it. He won't move fast enough, gasps for air, his balance lost. Behind us the tornado stalks, fixes on us, reads our minds. From somewhere inside itself it howls.

I pick my father up in my arms and slouch toward the cornfield. He is unbearably heavy and clings to me, digs his fingers into my shoulders, weeping. I put my mouth to his ear and tell him we're going to make it but I know we are not. With a single step the ground disappears beneath my feet and we fall into the ditch, skid to rest in a pool of runoff slime. I pull myself next to my father and lift his head up into my arms. Within seconds the black tube opens over us, consumes all light and sound but its own. I cover his body with mine, blanketing him not so much from the darkness that is about to take him but from the fear he will feel when it does.

* * *

My eyes open to a question: *What's that sound?* It's strained and constant, a tranquillized, phlegmy groaning. What makes sounds like that? My father used to. Sharing a room with him was a race to fall asleep first. If I lost he'd keep me up half the night with his gurglings, whistles, snorts and (most unsettling of all) his calls for help. In the last days when I moved a folda-way bed into his room to be close, the sounds he made in the night became grotesquely musical, a broken-down circus cal-liope. Anyway, it can't be him. It can't be anyone else, either. So it's me. I'm having a dream, the one about the tornado. I have to get one part of my brain to tell some other part to shut up, let it know I'm awake now, you can stop making those creepy sounds. And in a moment (a second? a minute or two?) it does. Then, at the same moment (or just before, or just after) there's the sound of a screen window being knocked in. A flimsy flip of metal springing away from its clips. Inside. Downstairs.

No. I don't know what it is, not for sure, but that's what I think it is. Somebody's breaking in. Then other explanations immediately parade their way through: a raccoon scrabbling at the garbage below the kitchen window, a shift in the house's foundations that unsettled the window frames, and yes, as always, it could just be the wind. This silent debate is carried on between the departments of my brain while I try to stay somewhere between sleep and alertness. I don't want to wake up all the way because that would give too much credit to what probably doesn't exist. Getting out of bed would only release those chemicals in your glands that create fear, the ones that make some people see a ghost in the way their shirt has been folded over a chair at the end of the bed. Nothing exists, not really, not until you wake up, turn on the lights and it's still there. Don't move, don't let whatever isn't there think you might be on to it. Better to play possum. Stay still, the sheets make too much noise. Listen. If you listen it will go away because it knows it's been heard. The problem is that after a while people go back to sleep, that's where they blow it. Bad things happen mostly to people about whom it is said they can sleep through anything.

There.

Definitely heard it that time, a creak of the floor too loud to be the wind. Footsteps in the kitchen, or heading for the kitchen. Somebody is in my house. Well, not my house, my father's house, although it can't really be said that it's his anymore, so it might as well be mine. Regardless, there is someone inside this house who did not use the usual routes of doorbell or key to get in. There's no returning to dreams of tornadoes now.

I get up slowly, careful that the bed doesn't creak, pull on a pair of track pants lying on the floor where I dropped them. Track pants: a great thing for the depressed, ill, or grieving. I'm not sure which I am, but that's part of what makes them great. They have been my best friends since the funeral, which saw me tightened up in a navy suit and my frayed university tie (the only one I hastily packed when I got the call). In the mirror that morning I looked slumped and pale, but collegiate and younger than I am, Holden Caulfield a few years later. Shaking the hands of mourners afterwards I wondered when I was going to be asked what I was planning to do after I graduated. The faces that bobbed by were my father's lawyer colleagues, a few golf buddies and their respective wives, the sort of vaguely familiar people who last shook my hand when I was twenty-three and heading off into the world (which for them wasn't a world at all but a particular set of career expectations). You didn't have to give anyone a real answer then. It was enough that you were male, had finished a degree, and hadn't yet attracted any lasting scandal. You'd passed. These were all the things you needed to go on to become one of them.

I tie a knot in the track pants and feel, in the darkness of my father's room, the vulnerable roll of belly fall over the tightened string. I'm not in bad shape, not in good shape, but I have the leftover pride of someone who used to be an athlete and still believes he can respond to the call if it ever comes. So I start to think that maybe this is it: an intruder in my father's house and me here alone to defend it. It's the sort of test he might have set up himself, the kind of thing that would translate nicely into a story of challenge and triumph. He was a good storyteller, could bring you in and have you laughing and flicking the tears away before you knew it, but he was always sure to sneak in the detail of his own personal victory or wise decision at the end. The message of his stories always seemed to be that life was unpredictable and hostile, but the right combination of strength and wit could overcome anything.

I slide over the hardwood floor and stand in the hallway, fine-tuning my hearing and sight. I expect to take on the hyper-alert senses of a cat (isn't that what happens to people standing in dark hallways?) but all I pick up is that it's dark. Darkness at 3:24 a.m. should come as no surprise, but it's still somehow more dark than I would've expected. How did I ever successfully get up, walk to the bathroom at the end of the hall and take a piss before without turning a light on in a house so dark?

I wish for night-lights. The pink plug-in kind that years ago seemed to fill the halls of other kids' homes whenever you had to find the toilet at a sleep-over party. My father had no idea such things existed, and would not have understood why anyone would buy them if he did. He was good at a few things (nobody would argue with the fact that he was effectively vicious on cross-examination in the courtroom, and elsewhere for that matter) but he was particularly good at resisting all things new. Whenever breakthroughs of science, political thought or the latest domestic convenience were explained to him he would open his eyes wide and scoff. That was the sort of person my father was. He scoffed a lot.

My father and night-lights. That's what I'm thinking of as I stretch and grasp for the wall in the surprising darkness. I'm wishing I had a childhood without shadows, a youth illuminated by pink bulbs glowing in the hallway. Maybe that way I'd have grown up to be the kind of man who lost no pride in keeping a light on all night now and then.

There.

The footsteps again, careful, searching. But the shoes are hard-soled and louder than a predator's should be. Don't burglars wear cross trainers now? Silent shoes, and good for a fence-scaling getaway? Whoever is in the living room hasn't thought of that, or doesn't care. I make my first steps to the top of the stairs, pleased by my own relative stealth.

Now what? There are two schools of thought on this. One acknowledges that burglars are often dangerous, heroin or crack freaks who will happily knife you in the gut for twenty bucks. Best thing to do is hide, call the cops if you can, and wait. The other line of thought prescribes going on the offensive. Grab something heavy, turn on the light and shout get-off-my-land threats. The problem here is that you have to be prepared to back it up with action.

I choose the second option. Maybe this is from taking care of 'things' lately. Sending cheques to florists and lawyers, being alone in the house you grew up in but have not been back to in seven years. A feeling that too much has happened from out of nowhere to sit back and let a stranger take something else away without a fight. But what was there to take? Nothing of mine was left, and it was never a house for heirlooms, trophies, portraits or souvenirs. It always had the feel of temporariness about it, of being a roof over heads. But it had been my parents' house and then my father's alone for almost thirty years. Somewhere during that time I lived here, too.

I pull air in through my mouth and hold, take the first steps down the stairs. The plan is to make it down to the front door where, beside the umbrellas and rubber boots, a garden spade leans against the wall waiting to be taken out to chip away the sidewalk ice. Then I'll flick on the light, wave it around and startle the bastard, send him out the same way he came. A good plan, I think. With just the right sprinkling of bravado, humour and humiliation. My father would have approved.

I take another step down and this time there's a creak, a terse denial of the wood: NO. I stop and listen for the footsteps to race over and check it out, but there's nothing. But nobody could have missed it, no mouse or squirrel between the walls could bring 170 pounds down in one step. Yet from where the footsteps sounded before there is silence.

I figure I'm about three more steps from the bottom and then from there fifteen feet to the door. *Move it!*, some reactivated voice in my brain tells me. *You're almost there, boy. Let's go!* It's the kind of voice you listen to. Even at the end my father had a voice like that. I tried to attribute it all to the fact that he was paid to make his voice deliver more meaning than the words alone carried. But sometimes, rarely and out of nowhere, he'd let the performance down and make you wonder if he was tired of keeping it up all his life. 'You're lonely,' he said to me from his bed, his words rubbery from the morphine the nurse and I kept pumping into him. 'Just like me. Your grandfather was a lonely man, too. It's in the genes.' I'd never thought of myself as lonely, as fated to be so, but when my father said it without resonance or bluster it sounded like a finally revealed truth.

Although I hear nothing, I decide it's time to move. I jump to the bottom of the stairs and land on the side of my feet, throwing myself off into the wall. By the time I straighten to make the last strides to the door I'm stopped by the sense that there is something in front of me that cannot be passed. There's also a whiff of machine oil, beer and musky deodorant. Then from out of the darkness what feels like a shovel but is in fact a fist clips across my chin.

My first thought is that I'm pleased the shot didn't knock me out immediately as I expected it would. In television, inexperienced fighters always go down with the first punch, and quite right too, their brain sloshed around like a sponge in a bucket. But here I am, standing. Head tilted over at an unlikely angle, a hot feeling in my testicles and speckles of blue light popping off before my eyes, but standing. *Now! Take a swing yourself!* But before I can send a message to my arm I take another shovel to the face, this time a straight ahead crunch to the nose. 'Give me some time!' I want to shout, but nothing comes out of my mouth except an alarming, involuntary gurgle. The instant bleeding from somewhere inside my skull bubbles down the back of my throat and tastes like Javex. Isn't blood supposed to taste like copper? That's what I heard somewhere but no, it's more like bleach or ammonia, or what you would imagine such poisons might taste like.

There's a sound of horseflies grinding in both my ears and my legs won't do as they're told. I'm not standing any more, I figure that much out. My feet are crumpled somewhere beneath me, and my back is slumped against the wall. *Get up! Don't let the bastard go!* But I can't see anything, even squinting it's too dark. With the help of the wall at my back I pull myself up and ready myself for another shovel to the skull while at the same time gauging where the front door might be, how many steps it would take to grab the spade, swing around and decapitate whatever it was that could see in the dark better than me.

FLINK. The front hall light is flicked on by a huge man wearing a shiny Maple Leafs jacket and black jeans with fancy orange stitching traced over his bulging thighs. The sudden light makes the details of him too much to take in all at once, especially his face. From the first glance I steal he looks older than me, somewhere in his thirties, with an expression of both anxiety and fatigue set around his eyes.

'I'm gonna leave, o.k.? Don't think about calling nobody till I'm gone, all right? And don't bother getting up. I'll see myself to the door,' he says, and exhales a single laugh.

He turns his back to me and I'm on him, clinging to his back. I've got his jacket, hold hard, try to pierce the material with my fingernails. But in the next second he's moving, all of his weight slugging toward the door, and the sickening blue lights are flashing in front of me like the ringside press gallery at a 1934 prize fight. But I can't let him go. This fucker broke into my father's house, suckerpunched me into something near a coma and now he's making for the front door, leaving by the proper route like he's got a right to. I've got him though, and I'm hanging on. He can drag me to his car, blow my head off, drop me in the trunk and fling me off a sideroad bridge but I'm hanging on.

But he's big, bigger than you'd ever guess, and his jacket is slippery nylon. My hand gives way and drops to the floor, giving his wide ass an encouraging football player slap on the way down. When he makes it to the door he spends a moment figuring out how to unlock it. My father went for elaborate dead-bolts, digital combinations and chains. He had an ongoing account and was on a first-name basis with his locksmith. Both would have had a good laugh over the fact that the only burglar the house has ever known is having a harder time getting out than he did getting in.

'This is my father's house,' I tell the burglar, and realize my mouth is even with the floor, my breath blowing balls of dust across the wood slats like tumbleweed.

'Shit, man, give it up,' he says, and pulls the door open with a dramatic swing. Give what up? My father? The house?

I pull myself up once more. I'm still under the impression I can get this guy, pull him down, pull him back. But I'm crazy with dizziness, a fish in my head that doesn't want to be there and is too big to fit.

I lunge for him but my cheek catches the end of the door, cuts out a flap of my face. Still I grab for him, not a clue in my head.

'Come back!' I gurgle, but he's already down the wooden porch stairs and onto the front walk. He looks from side to side, checks for traffic or curious neighbours sticking their nose out from the curtains. He must feel safe because he turns, puts his hands on his hips in a gesture of domestic exhaustion, as though he just finished doing the dishes and someone brought in a forgotten stack of dirty ones from the living room. 'Get over it. Just get *over* it,' he says. His voice is not entirely without sympathy.

Then he turns again and runs, but not really. More like a jog, his arms lolling loose at his sides, not going anywhere fast. It's the way loss moves: Deliberate, unhurried, smug.

He's gone and I just missed him. I tried, I really tried. But I just missed him.

'Come back!' I scream out the front door of my father's house long after the thief has run out of sight, out of range of sound. Slumped on the front step, blowing snotblood out of nose and mouth, calling out like a tearful drunk into the indifferent night.

'Come back! Come back!'

Magnificent

WHEN THEY RELEASED my father from the hospital after his stroke we put him in the guest bedroom on the top floor, so he could look out the window over the fields. Through the fake lace curtains his land spread out from the line of the concession road to the Van Dorsens' distant silos. According to my mother, though, he never turned his head to look. All that winter he lay beneath the blankets she would heap unnecessarily upon him, moaning when he was hungry or had to be helped to the bathroom. The first few days he tried to speak, but his lazy tongue and fallen lips could not form any of the words he wanted, and soon he gave up altogether.

I drove out from the city to visit almost every weekend, and my mother would greet me with hopeful news, some evidence of improvement: 'You know, yesterday he sort of sat up on his own when I brought in his lunch,' or, 'When I told him you would be here for dinner he nodded his head, and I'd say he smiled. He can't talk, but he can still smile!' When he died later in March the snow was retreating into earth-veined patches in the fields. 'He didn't hang on until spring,' my mother said to me when she called to tell me. 'He might've been happier if we could have opened up his window for the spring.'

I moved my mother to Toronto from the farm so she could be nearby, and so that she didn't have to live entirely on her own. The idea was that I'd take time off from my workaholic routine and spoil her with Holt Renfrew shopping sprees, Sunday dinners at whatever hot new restaurants were written up that week, tickets to the megamusicals that rolled in and out of town. It would add up to a better life than what she would have if she stayed on the farm, where I assumed she would be lonely and find it a struggle to manage the day-to-day operations. I imagined that if she stayed every corner of the old house would hold for her some difficult episode or image from the past. Every April-flooded basement and crooked

Christmas tree, every fight with my father which ended in slammed doors and shouted promises of divorce, all of my illegal crayon wall drawings (now covered with wildflower wallpaper) would come out at her, voices sounding up from the red brick foundation. I foresaw peeling paint, concerned calls from neighbours, Meals on Wheels.

She lived in Toronto only three years before she too died, but I see her life there as impossibly extended. A grey pattern of small domestic tasks, television, long moments gazing out the apartment window at the crawling activity on the streets below. She declined most of the plans I would make for her, politely, and tell me not to worry, she was fine, just fine. And so it is that I remember the end of her life as a whole other lifetime. One that went on in a state of absence, without narrative, notice or event.

* * *

When she first came to Toronto my mother and I spent our mornings looking through pictures of condo projects in the real estate section. Places with important-sounding descriptions and names borrowed from old English estates told us that we would be missing a very special opportunity if we did not 'explore' their 'new world of living'. I asked what was important to her: was she bothered by the idea of a high-rise, or would she prefer a flat in a renovated Victorian? She said she didn't mind, they all looked very nice. I told her that some of these buildings had indoor pools, exercise rooms where they held group aerobic classes for seniors, activities nights through the week. She said she doubted she would be in any hurry to do those kinds of things with strangers.

On the weekend and some of the evenings I would drive her around to see some of the buildings. Sometimes we would park and go in as far as their mirror-walled lobbies, to stand beneath the icicle-glass chandelier. 'Well, well,' my mother would say absently to the brass door handles, tuxedoed doorman or impossibly huge potted trees.

'What about this place?' I would ask her.

'I wonder who they get to come in to water all those plants.'

I see my mother before the window over the kitchen sink in our old house. It is winter: outside the fields lie in sun-reflecting whiteness. On the sill there are blue bottles that once contained wine vinegar but now stand empty, the sunlight passing through them in watercolour shafts. She wears a red striped shirt of my father's rolled up past her elbows and open wide at her freckled neck. Her skin and clothes smell of dish detergent and cigarette smoke. She is telling me about the year she lived in Dublin when she was a girl. She was there to go to college, to learn to be a nurse.

'I was only a wee thing, I don't know, I guess I would be seventeen or eighteen. We would work all day and late into the night. At class in the morning and doing rounds with the sister the rest of the time. And afterwards we would go out to the dance halls or see the last half of a play if they had extra seats and then be up for eight o'clock the next morning. We were crazy then! Go, go, go! Never stopped!' She shakes her head and looks at me, as if even now she can't believe it all. But it doesn't sound like something she particularly misses, either. There is no edge of sadness in her words, or even dreamy nostalgia. Just an amused, head-shaking wonder.

'And the doctors were always asking us out. They had no other chance to meet girls, you see, they were always working in the hospital. But they were great fun, taking you here and there. In those days people just went out like that, they didn't take things so seriously. We didn't talk about marriage until we had to, until you were ready or had gotten in trouble. Then you had to, of course, but I suppose today you don't have to do anything you don't want. We never had those choices to make, so we just had as much fun as we could for the time.'

She never married one of the doctors, although she said she was always asked, over and over. Sitting at the kitchen table I would ask her why she never accepted. 'Oh no. No, no,' she would say, her back to me and her hands in the sink. She said it as if their proposals were only ridiculous jokes. 'You see, they were only having their fun with me.'

Instead, after she had gotten her nurse's certificate, she moved back to the family farm in Donegal. There she met my father at her sister's wedding. He was in the wedding party, the groom's best friend. Soon after, they too got married, and not much later moved to Canada. The reasons for their emigration, or the details of their courtship were never made clear to me. It was as if her youth ended in that one moment, the first dance with my father at her sister's wedding. She would recall their foxtrotting and jitterbugging together after the band had left and been replaced by a single-speaker phonograph playing Sinatra, but that was it. The stories of Ireland, eccentric family characters and wicked girls' games would end there, with his hands around her waist in the front room of the town's only hotel, shuffling to the tinny sound of American brass. 'Chicago, New York! What did we know of those places Sinatra would sing about?' she would laugh and go no further. After that, it seemed her life stopped being so insanely full of activity. The stories of spontaneity and foolishness were replaced by episodes in my growing up, the condition of her perennials, the scandals of neighbours' families, and the relative ferocity of the blizzards of '67, '74 and '86.

* * *

We decided finally on one place, based on its promise of 'huge terraces overlooking splendid parks'. I wondered where such land existed in Toronto, but kept any such questions to myself. We booked a viewing time with a sales agent named Anthony Rose. I told him over the phone that his name sounded very distinctive, but I immediately regretted it. It came to me that I had borrowed my adjective from the condo's ad for *distinctive* residences.

'Well! Thank you!' he said with an almost theatrical false modesty, delivered in a nobody's-ever-noticed-before tone. And then softer, in a confiding whisper, 'But you know, let me tell you, it's not my real name. I just made it up. But I like it!'

When we arrived at the building, Anthony Rose was there to greet us. I remember he talked a lot, and he wore a beautiful, expensive-looking suit. 'How are you today, madam? Ready for a little tour?' he said to my mother, bending over at the waist to level his smiling head upon her. She nodded and worked up a difficult smile herself. Then he took her unnecessarily by the arm into his clean and bookless office, where he offered us coffee and doughnuts. 'Actually, my mother and I prefer tea,' I told Anthony Rose. 'Oh you know, so do I!' he said, but did not get us any. Instead he moved us out to be taken around the main floor, to see the 'lifestyle amenities' before going up to the condo itself. As we moved down the silent hallways that smelled of new carpet and varnish, Anthony Rose kept urging us to poke our faces into different rooms, each of which offered some luxury, service or ornament. By now his talking was mostly addressed to me, particularly when he spoke of money. He didn't think my mother would be able to understand the meaning of the figures, the urgency of the situation which they implied.

'So, as I told you, this unit is now priced at one-sixty-two-seven, but I can't say it'll be around for long. Not at *that* price. We have a couple other layouts available at this point, but if you don't mind my saying, I think this one best suits the needs of your Ma.'

The needs of my Ma. 'Needs' meant old age, fragility, the desire to be close to a hospital. 'Ma' meant people from the country: ordinary, decent, a little senseless.

'This seems like her sort of place,' he added after a moment of apparent thought, as if sincerely considering its suitability.

I wondered, watching the look of laboured interest on my mother's face, if he could possibly be more wrong.

* * *

I see my mother digging around in the flower bed that lay beneath the front picture window at our old house. In the summer, in the few hours after dinner and before dark, she would come out and work in that muddy square that she enlarged each spring until it crept around the other side of the house and almost out to the drive. Usually I would come out with her, sometimes to help, but mostly to sit on the brick step and talk, or just gaze out in a daydream fog. She never seemed to mind my being there, even if I sat in silence.

When we talked, we talked about little things. How strange and sort of sad it was that the morning glory would bloom only once, or how much the sound of the cicada was like an electric generator's hum. Once, the summer before my first year of university, she asked me if I would ever come back here. I told her I didn't know what she meant.

'Will you ever come back here to work the farm? Like when your father gets too old to do it himself,' she explained with her knees at the base of a rose bush.

'No. I don't think so,' I remember answering without a thought, without even considering the potential for insult. For the truth of it was, I knew the farm was a place I would leave and avoid looking back upon, I was certain of that even at the time. But my mother went right back to the branch she was pruning without pause, without drama.

'No, you wouldn't,' she said without turning her head. 'What would you do if you did?'

* * *

As Anthony Rose showed her the apartment's small assets, switches and kitchen conveniences, my mother maintained a look of keen interest. Everything he said appeared to be impressing her more and more. This was a fancy showcase, an exhibition at the CNE showing how we might live a century from now. But there it all was being offered to her now: the food disposal, dimmer switches, the silver-doored garbage chute that, when opened, exhaled a warm, papery breath from six floors below. The whole time my mother said little except, at the moments she felt obliged to be impressed, she used the same word over and over. 'Magnificent!' she said.

I had never heard her use it before. The word itself seemed to her a welcome discovery, something to hold on to. It functioned as a bridge between herself and the person she believed should be here, an accomplished woman being guided through the luxurious rewards of her work, her life. If my father was there he would've been too busy pointing out all the inadequacies and useless expenses to allow my mother a chance for comment. But now she was alone. This would be hers alone.

As we moved before the bare picture windows which framed the bundle of downtown office towers, she moved her head from side to side, as if carefully checking everything out. Her lips were tight and pale from the work of maintaining an unmoving smile. 'Magnificent!' she said to nobody in particular as we stepped silently through the sterile rooms of off-white walls and grey carpet. The space absorbed us, leaving my mother's unlikely word to fill every vacant corner. Again and again its royal syllables were formed by her thin, colourless lips.

'Magnificent!' she said. 'Oh yes, magnificent!'

The Author Shows a Little Kindness

FOR A LONG TIME she tried to write one of those knockout opening sentences: unexpected, diamond-perfect, a taste of the narrative's past and a foreshadow of its future. Her inability to write anything of the sort frustrated her at first but was a comfort later when she gave up on art altogether. She took a night course called 'Better Writing, Better You' that worked to release what the teacher kept calling the Voice, but her hopeless struggle over the first sentence convinced her that her own Voice was not in the least interested in being heard. Instead, she found that her decision to see the world as it is, in grey shades and without make-up, helped rid her of what her now married schoolgirl friends would have called 'fancy ideas'. She told herself that if life itself isn't made up of clever, rhythmic, startling sentences, it was dishonest for her to try to make it that way. Who was *she* to write the story of her life? What got into her that made her think she could make her own banalities and prejudices sing in lyrical paragraphs that would lead to a hint at some universal truth or other? Who did she think she was? At any rate, the notion eventually left her and took with it the vividness of the story she would have told, the sharp edges of her memory. But there was consolation even in this, in the relief of avoiding a course that would have led to self-exposure and embarrassment. She can smile now at the arrogance behind her efforts toward not only writing but (far worse) seeing herself as 'a writer' too.

If she (her name is Mary – a name she has always resented for its summoning of bosomy nuns) were ever able to kickstart the story of her life she would have tried, once and for all, to get her childhood confusions and loose ends straightened out and tied up. Her father's affair with her mother's sister, her mother's strained efforts to hide her knowledge of it, the elementary school English teacher whom Mary loved and showed her secret poems to but who turned abruptly away from her to prevent himself 'from going too far'. All of this, the difficult connections and implications, this was the interesting material of Mary's story, as far as she saw it. The later stuff, the contemporary events – who would ever care about that? A degree in sociology from the University of Guelph, then straight into a counselling job with Children's Aid in Peterborough (sad work and with fewer satisfactions than might be imagined) and, after somewhere between a few and many years of non-event, that is where she lies today. Not 'lies' (she isn't dead – not yet dead) but lives, or at least, it's the place where she has found herself settled. An apartment off Water Street close enough to a Loblaw's, dry cleaners and video rental place that she's never needed to buy a car, which is just as well because she could never afford one and, to be truthful, she's never needed to go anywhere else anyway.

After her thirty-second year came and went with a long distance rendition of 'Happy Birthday' from her parents (still together) and a self-reward of Double Chocolate Brownie Delight straight out of the tub, a tide of dissatisfaction began rising within her, more a numbing of the senses than anything like despair. Mary found herself considering changes, making a move, taking up hobbies. The creative writing workshop came first. Then she applied to go back for a master's degree. But her memories of university (listening to drunk jocks roar and piss outside her window, ominous shouts and poundings through the walls, the smell of vomit rising from the dorm carpet) would always rise to challenge her imagined world of books, leafy quads and inspired all-nighters. Every idea that occurred to her could be boiled down to little more than inconveniences, risks of failure and stressful atmospheres.

So now, there she is: Mary. A woman in mid-career, caught in the mid-swing of attempted transformation, sliding without interruption into middle age. There is so much 'middle' about her these days (middle of her class grown thick around the middle) that she cannot fully recall the sensation of standing at the edges, of imagining yourself as an exception to the rule. It cannot even be said that she is waiting for something to happen. To wait in this way requires that this 'something' is going to come, maybe later for her than others, but it is surely on its way. The thing is that Mary is not so sure any more that her waiting has a purpose. These days she's noticed she yearns less, suffers loneliness less, feels the apartment's silence less. But not because these things have been replaced by contentment. Something else has moved in to take their place, a resignation that has sheared off her edges and replaced them with the suspicion that perhaps waiting is all there is.

* * *

What does Mary look like? Some people need to know such things before they can move ahead with a story, like Mary's own mother, whose habit was to stop and ask 'What *kind* of woman was she?' whenever another's name was mentioned. To this end let's just say that Mary was grateful for the winter. It saved her from the humiliations of having to tuck her backside into knee-length, perpetually unfashionable shorts and the self-consciousness of her breasts shifting and leaping inside over-sized cotton T-shirts. Summer was nothing but a prolonged magnification of her largeness. Winter, on the other hand, offered her the chance to take up residence inside knit sweaters, to let their thoughtful colours and designs speak for her. Standing before mirrors she could even accept herself as warm-looking, someone you could imagine living comfortably in a cabin deep in the woods. She couldn't see a beautiful woman in her reflection but 'a good woman,' a wife from pioneer days, pleasing to have around kitchens and under the covers in chilly bedrooms.

When Cliff first saw Mary he thought she had a pretty face although it was a shame she had let herself go a bit in other regions. But within minutes he found that he noticed her heaviness less and her pretty face more. These improvements were reinforced by the reminder that none of us are perfect and that things, all things, as Cliff knew, could be worse.

Cliff was a new client of Mary's, just moved to Peterborough three months ago. His regular check-ins were a condition of his Young Offender's parole. The first thing Mary noticed was that he was tall and slim, a body shape you might think of calling 'wiry' but it wouldn't be quite right. It's more that he had a short trunk and long limbs, but they were thick and strong, and looked not at all like wires. When he walked into her office he bent low at the hips to shake Mary's hand.

'Hello, Cliff,' she said, relieved to hear her voice has maintained its calm, counsellor's tone.

'Hey,' he says, and sits.

'How are things?'

'All right. Not bad. Whatever.'

The second thing Mary notices about Cliff is that his face is stern. But more. It's accusatory, a pointed finger. A face that suggests a man – a young man – who prefers the silent company of big, energetic dogs to human beings. Although she recognizes the difficulty in this, she finds his expression not at all unpleasant to be faced with.

Mary lowers her eyes to the pages in front of her, fingers the leathery paper of Cliff's file. It is thick with social worker reports, therapists' letters, transfer memos and a three-page 'dope sheet' of criminal convictions, both indictable and petty. A handful of thefts, two unlawful possessions of a firearm, eight failures to appear, one escaping detention, and a half-dozen assaults. Mary re-checks his age: 19. But there has been no new offence since his last release date over six months ago, and the latest memo from the Toronto office noted, simply, 'Sporadic employment. Apparent improvement in outlook/disposition.'

'You've had a busy time of it, from what I see,' she says, and reminds herself to not shake her head as she does so. It's the sort of thing she's caught herself doing from time to time for effect, but she can see how someone could resent it as a gesture of judgement.

'Busy, but not so busy. It doesn't take long to mess shit up. Sorry, I mean mess things up.'

Mary smiles up at him briefly, hoping to excuse him. She tries to communicate *You can say what you like with me* with her eyes.

'Well, about your criminal history, our concern is that –'

'I've given up on all that,' he interrupts. His tone doesn't indicate any willed self-reform, but just what he says: *I've given up on all that.*

Cliff sighs as Mary closes his file and looks at him from across her undersized desk. How many files with his name on them had he seen closed in just that way over the years? How many administrators, doctors, therapists and police had asked him to explain himself? Many of them had made honest attempts at actually helping, but as it turned out he hadn't changed his ways on account of any of their efforts. He had just become finally, overwhelmingly tired. Tired of the institutions, of their offices, waiting rooms, bleached marble hallways and living rooms with three-year-old magazines and a too-small TV lodged in the corner.

If he had a way with words, any kind of confidence or cleverness with them at all, Cliff would have said that he was sorry for the pain he'd caused all the people who'd tried to care for him but were prevented by his hatred of their trying. It was far too late for these words, he knew that, but he wished for them nevertheless, and how he would use them to tell them all about how nothing was any of their fault, not a thing. They weren't the ones who left him, four months old, wrapped in a *Sunday Star* beside the automatic sliding doors of the Toronto General. They, the ones afterwards, had meant him well and in return he had wished them dead. Was it that he had no heart at all? No, he'd tell them today, in this imaginary speech he would give if he had even the slightest skill in finding the right words. No, but I think I do now. I want to have one now.

'I'm glad to hear you're making changes,' Mary says.

'Things change on their own,' Cliff answers, keeping his eyes on hers. 'That's the way it's always been with me.'

Mary feels, despite the generation that sits between them, that she knows just what he means. She appreciates his honesty and admires his gentle, premature, life-hardened fatigue. But not 'admires'. That can't be the right word. For how can she merely admire the thing that leads her into love?

* * *

On his third visit to Mary's office after the usual questions and answers Cliff did something extraordinary: without changing the setting of his face, without raising an eyebrow or the corners of his lips, he reached his hand across the desk and covered hers, formed a warm shell over her knuckles and veins. An easy way to describe this moment of contact would be to say 'it happened automatically' or 'without his thinking', but as is the case with the most simple and often used explanations, it would not be wholly true. He had thought about it, if a sudden idea can be called 'thought'. And as for Mary, Cliff's touch was at once surprising and came as no surprise at all. The touch made her thighs tremble, but she did not move her hand away for a long while.

That night, after tiptoeing up the stairs past Mrs Lambert's door (the landlady, who spoke of sex as though it were grounds for eviction) they made love tenderly, but not so tenderly that the vigour and uncomplicated gratification was taken out of it. They made love well, they would have agreed on that, if they had spoken openly about it. They made love tenderly and well all through their first night together, and in the morning they ate microwaved leftover pizza in bed and slept curled close to each other in the shape of two semi-colons under the sheet.

In spite of this new comfort, the first thing Mary said to Cliff when words returned to her was, 'There's gonna be hell to pay for this.' Conflict of interest, unprofessional conduct, exposure to potential liability, small-town moral expectation. Whatever the ultimate reason, whether it's written somewhere or not, a social worker cannot fall in love with a teenaged client on criminal probation in Peterborough, Ontario.

But caution, as is so often the case in such adventures, was not enough. Maggie McTaggart, the witchy, older-than-the-hills director of the office, sniffed Mary out almost immediately. Like a cat in the spring, Maggie McTaggart became prickly, her back raised in strange arches, her whiskers picking up both troubling and arousing signals. Within a single day what would previously have been offered as gentle criticisms became blasting tantrums. Nothing, suddenly, was right: too much, too little, too fast, too slow. Accusations of laziness echoed after sly, suggestive whisperings. 'I could use a little *help* around here,' she would shout from her office with dramatic exasperation and only Mary around to hear, or hiss '*Somebody's* got the glow on,' with a unfriendly smile, from around the corner of Mary's door. Overnight the office, which was really just a single room with three desks separated by flimsy fibreglass walls, became a discomfiting theatre of conflict, treachery and double meanings. A bleakly staged melodrama with everybody getting increasingly upset over a central, but buried, secret.

To make matters worse, by way of small-town coincidence, Maggie McTaggart's friend and thrice-a-week lunch partner was none other than Mary's landlady, Mrs Lambert. Together they made a suspicious, even hateful pair. Having joined them once or twice for grilled cheeses at the Woolco lunch counter Mary knew they spoke never of themselves and always of others, and rarely with any kindness.

'It's a shame about Jim Bradshaw's MS, isn't it? Can't eat or wipe himself on his own, I hear,' Maggie McTaggart once began, flagging the counter girl down for another lemon slice and more hot water in her tea.

'A shame. But it probably serves him right for all those years he walked around like a proud old cock. And after what happened with that cleaning lady, the poor little Greek girl.'

'It's all probably taught him a few things about knowing your place. Your place under God, you know?'

'It's awful, it shouldn't happen to anyone. But I think you're absolutely right,' Mrs Lambert said, clicked her fingers for the bill and rummaged in her purse for an inadequate tip. That was the kind of ladies they were.

In the end, neither Maggie McTaggart's warning signs, Mrs Lambert's priggishness nor Mary's own prudence prevented Cliff from moving into her apartment. It was accomplished over a course of meetings and under conditions of elaborate stealth (one plan involved a flashlight signalling the all-clear from her bedroom window, another a dangerous climb up the drainpipe). The physical moving in did not happen all at once, but incrementally, one gym bag of clothes, ghettoblaster, and box of paperbacks at a time. Cliff moved in without asking if he could or whether Mary thought it wise, and when the day finally came when he cancelled the lease on his other place, she was pleased he hadn't. She was glad of his presumption and the way it relieved her of having to think about starting what she would have thought to be (if she allowed herself to think of it) an impossible life together.

And then Mary made a mistake. A moment where she allowed her mind to close and granted her body an extravagance: in their bed, two floors above where Mrs Lambert struggled to find sleep in her stale-perfume, too-hot room, Mary called out. Then came long and wavering screams, then cries, then whimpers. Her face bliss-twisted, her muscles loose and sweet, Mary made sounds she had heard here and there in certain movies but had never before made herself. But they were not imitations. Her song was entirely and involuntarily her own. Below the labouring floorboards, in a flush of anger and shame and regret, Mrs Lambert concluded that there could be no circumstance whereby a woman, however expert, could reach such heights all on her own.

'She must have heard that,' she said to Cliff, clinging to his muscled neck.

'What does it matter?'

'It matters.'

'You can do whatever you want. You're a big girl.'

'I'm big. But I can't get away with everything.'

This turned out to be true. Two days later Mary was asked if she could, when she had a spare moment, come round to Maggie McTaggart's desk for a chat. There was something false about the way 'chat' fell wearily, ruefully from her mouth. Mary decided then that if this was the day she was to be fired she might as well go on the offensive. It was a position she wasn't used to, and as she slid her hips around the photocopier and lumped herself into the chair before the old lady she felt hot and fuzzy with the blood of recklessness.

'It has come to my attention,' Maggie McTaggart began, her head raised as though dictating a business letter, 'that you are engaged in intimate relations with a client. Cliff Rathmuller. Is this so?'

'Is that what your spy told you?'

'Is it true?'

'Yes. He's a consenting adult, you know.'

'That's true, under the law, strictly speaking. But Mary, really, I don't want to seem a *prude*. But we provide a *community* service ...'

'We're not running a fucking church.'

'Beg pardon?'

Mary stood and leaned over the desk, bared a threatening glimpse of rosy cleavage. 'What I said was: This is not a fucking church.'

'That may be,' Maggie McTaggart replied, clenched and even. 'But there seems to be altogether too much fucking going on here, nevertheless.'

Good for you, Mary thought. The old bag's got a bit of piss and vinegar left in her yet.

'For this reason and the obvious ways it presents a conflict of interest, as well as for the way it prevents you from performing your tasks according to minimum standards, you are hereby dismissed.'

'Can you do this?' Mary asks, immediately regrets it, and wonders at how quickly her exhilarating rush of defiance has drained away.

'Yes, indeed. I can do this. In fact I believe I just did.'

And then Maggie McTaggart, in a gesture borrowed from Katherine Hepburn, lifted her wrinkled chin in triumph.

* * *

One morning, a couple of months after Mary's severance money had run out and the credit card collection agency had begun calling every day at 8:10 a.m., Cliff woke Mary by lifting her head up in his hands and, before her eyelids lifted from the weight of sleep, told her, 'I got some money. We're going to leave today.'

'How much?' she asked him through her grogginess, although the question that was first in her head was, 'Where to?'

'Enough.'

She ate a bowl of cereal, packed her only suitcase half full and was sitting next to Cliff, pulling out of the apartment building's driveway in a car she had never seen before all in under half an hour.

'It's a nice car,' she said, touching his arm.

'It's German,' he nodded. 'Forest green.'

'Forest green. It's nice.'

Then she fell asleep, and when she woke she was in a town she had heard of but never been to before in her life. There were streets with full-grown trees lining their sides, a downtown with a barber shop, a butcher's window garlanded with sausages, a movie theatre that had not yet been divided up into smaller theatres and a bookstore that displayed a copy of her favourite Canadian author's latest in the window. She liked the place. She liked it fine.

They found an apartment at an amazingly low rent on the second floor of a house owned by somebody Cliff knew. 'Not a friend,' he explained when Mary asked more specific questions. 'We just lived together once. Before.' And Mary knew this meant when Cliff was a bad man who knew bad men in bad places.

Sometime during their first days in the new apartment when Cliff was out buying a square-head screwdriver and a shelf for the bathroom Mary watched something on TV about a bank robbery in Peterborough: largest take in fourteen years. Nobody hurt although a gun was waved by a single man in a ski mask. Massive manhunt in effect. Police have no present leads. Reward offered for information leading to an arrest and conviction.

At the commercial Mary turned the TV off, pulled out the plug, wrapped the cord into a neat coil and slid it below the rug.

* * *

As it turned out, Mary's first impression that Cliff was more a 'dog person' than a 'people person' was correct. This fact, combined with their decision that it was irresponsible for him and too late in the game for her to have children, led them to keep dogs instead. Shining black Labradors, never less than two at a time. Over the years some of them, according to canine custom, crawled under the porch or away altogether in the night in order to die. But these deaths came always after at least a hundred dog years of deliriously fetched sticks, Milk-Bones, scratched bellies and a rug at the end of the bed. Mary brushed and fed them and Cliff took them for walks through the cemetery after work (he'd found a job delivering meals at the hospital). When he came home he would find her at the kitchen table writing in her journal, filling up the pages with tightly packed paragraphs cut by intermittent columns of dialogue. He kept quiet until she was finished. She seemed to go somewhere else when she was writing and he remembered hearing somewhere that it was dangerous to wake sleepwalkers. If you interrupted them you could leave them in a permanent dream. But when she put down her pen she was fine again, refreshed and energized, placing the journals above the stove next to the Yellow Pages and *Fanny Flagg's Farmhouse Cooking*. Only once did Cliff ask what Mary wrote about, and her answer satisfied him enough that he never had to ask again. 'It's the story of a sad woman who gets a chance to be happy,' she said, closed the cover shut and raised herself wholly into his arms.

Once she took a real run at it Mary's first sentence had been easily written, and it was a good one, too. Many others came after, each one holding on to the tail of the one before it like a string of circus elephants, a parade of trained performers passing before her eyes. They started in the past and moved forward, backtracking and meandering, spiralling in on the present. She lingered over the mechanics of her story, melted herself into the detail, the unexpected factors that had brought her to the life of a bank robber's wife, to contentment, to love. But she knew that it couldn't be finished, not ever. She knew that some day she'd have to answer the questions that rose in her head whenever she imagined her own particular version of the 'happily ever after': What happens now, Mary? What happens next?

X-Ray

YOU SHOULD KNOW that the lead apron we put on only protects you from 80 per cent of the radiation. Even less if you need a series of exposures, like if you broke your legs, fractured your skull and cracked your ribs after a car crash or similar trauma. We see a lot of that. Trauma, that is.

And then there's the lifers, the ones we have to monitor for changes, enlargements, new growths. They're in here so much that half the time we're probably *causing* cancer. And this despite the fact that throughout our clinical training we're told about the importance of keeping the number of sessions to a minimum. But I still haven't met an X-ray technician who keeps track. I sometimes wonder why some of my patients, the terminals, don't get pushed out of Radiology glowing nuclear yellow under their white cotton bedclothes. They wouldn't stop bringing them in, though. They always need to know more, to look inside. It's necessary to look inside to know what's wrong.

* * *

I could say that my boyfriend beats me, but I prefer to call them fights. Fights he wins, of course, but that's still the way I see them. Sometimes he starts them, sometimes me, but he always gets the last word. It's hard to talk when your mouth is full of blood and the tears tighten your lungs and make you choke.

I love him, though. He's a good man. And I'm not one of those stupid women you always hear about who cling to their men out of desperation or fear. He really *is* good. There's never any real damage, anyway. Nothing broken, no internal haemorrhaging. Usually you can't tell when a face has been slapped into a coffee table from an X-ray.

There was probably a time I wouldn't have put up with any of Glen's shit. But who can be the person they used to be? My mother told me that it's hard to judge the man you live with, and she was right. Love's the thing that makes you lose the clarity of distance, all the issues get fuzzy. I've learned to forgive, although that's not quite the right word for it. It's more like just *going on*. Like when I found out Glen was fucking somebody else.

Underwear. Right out of one of those trash novels on the supermarket racks. It's always underwear that gives people away in those books. Panties being left under the bed, tucked into jacket pockets, stuffed into gloveboxes. There was a time when it was lipstick on the collar. Now its sick, sweet, dainty little panties. In my case it was somewhat different, however. With me it was *his* underwear, or actually the lack of them. He just came home late one night, with me already in bed pretending to sleep, took off his pants and there he was, in the buck. He'd put them on this morning (the ones with 'LET'S PARTY!' on the back and arrows pointing to the front slit) and now they were gone.

I snapped on the light. There was nothing that could be taken as guilt in his slack eyes but he stopped and faced me anyway, expecting something. His penis hung there pink and thick from whatever work it had been up to a couple of hours before he came home to our bed.

'Who is it?'

'What?'

'Who are you doing it with? Donna? The one with the tits?'

'Don't start. You're nuts. Paranoid.'

'Stop fucking with me. Who is it?'

'What do you want? Do you really want to know?'

Yes. No.

'Do you make her say all the things you want? Or are you only a pervert with me?'

'Just drop it, OK? I'm too tired to get pissed off.'

I turn off the bedside light and try to be decisive and angry about the way I do it, but it's not the same as slamming a door or breaking a plate.

When he came into bed he stayed to his side but I could smell the whisky. Not cheap rye either. Chivas or one of those ten-year-old Scotches with the strange names. Must have been somebody fancy. Only at weddings or Christmas (when I bought him a bottle) would he drink the good stuff. With me it's always beer.

'We'll talk about it tomorrow. Christ, I'm tired,' he says and goes to sleep. A couple minutes later, he farts. Just lets one go without an excuse me. That was almost the worst part.

But I let him sleep.

It only strikes me the next morning, when I'm sticking up some exposures for Dr. Sullivan of a woman with ovaries the size of tennis balls, that it must have been the other woman who'd made him so tired, and I didn't get to say a word about that at the time. But you can't bring things like that up the day after they're said. Even though you're right, you just end up sounding like a bitch if you do.

* * *

There's this one patient at the hospital, Mr. Donoghue. He's dying, everybody knows it. 'Riddled with secondaries,' Dr. Lefebvre says to me whenever he studies the exposures I put up for him, and I picture his cancer as an actual riddle, a puzzle inside of him so complex that a solution is beyond the best of us. Mr. Donoghue's a sweet man, though, and funny. A lot of them are like that, when they get close to the end. They see the whole thing as a joke, or at least they make jokes about it. Either they're like that or they're terrified, desolate, leaked-out party balloons. It's one or the other.

The other day I was getting him ready for another X-ray, moving his legs onto their side, raising his chin into a plastic cup to hold his head still, moving his arm up behind his neck to show the pronounced ridges of his ribs.

'You're tying me up and we haven't even had a drink first,' he says.

'I move fast.'

'I bet you do.'

There's a smile, but it trembles at the edges. He's going. Every time I see him now something new has left him, a basic skill has been lost. As if sensing me noticing this, he sighs. I watch his bony chest rise and fall in what seems to take a full minute.

'I'm tired of this,' he says.

'I know. Just work with me.'

'Why?'

'We need a few more takes. Got to get all the right angles.'

'What does it matter?'

'I don't know. It probably doesn't.'

We're not supposed to say things like that, we've been instructed to be hopeful and light. But it was true, and it seems disrespectful to lie to somebody who knows full well they are going to die in a hospital being shuttled around to different rooms and placed before various machines.

'Go ahead then,' he says, and closes his eyes. 'I'll do it for you, sweetheart.'

As I move his body around to get it into the right positions, he holds the same weird smile on his face the whole time. It's like he's flirting, but the idea is ridiculous. His face is collapsed, the skin of his body on the table grey and translucent like a plastic bag. How can he desire anything at this point looking like that? Then again, why the hell not?

'Thank you,' I tell him. 'You're *so* good to me.'

Then he says something in a tone that is flat and serious, as if he's already a ghost making a promise from the other side.

'I'll remember you,' he says.

* * *

When Glen and I first started going out together he had trouble with his erections. The trouble was that he never got them, of if he did he kept them to himself. This was six years ago when we were both of an age that I assumed sex was a done deal, if not expertly then satisfactorily mastered, and all the mechanical bugs pretty much ironed out. Glen was also the kind of guy you'd never expect those kind of problems with. He had a deep voice and broad shoulders and big hands.

We tried games. Mind games. The kind of thing most people try after a while, just for a change. It started as my suggestion because Glen would only storm out of the room at the mention of counselling or doctors and he didn't seem much interested in exploring any home remedies of his own. So we tried the usual things: Hot Secretary, Runaway Teen, Stepdaughter, Geisha Girl, Little Sister. Always me in character

‹ 116 ›

acting in a vacuum and Glen playing himself, silent and tense and shrunken on the bed. None of them seemed to kindle his imagination or anything else, and my dressing up and dirty talk came to anger him so much that he would get up and lock himself in the bathroom for a couple of hours and tell me to go fuck myself when I called through the door to ask if he was all right.

Then we struck upon Mommy. All the other roles seemed conventional and hokey and a little embarrassing to perform, but playing mother had to be the most clichéd of them all. While there seemed to be an edge of something 'wrong' and 'perverse' about acting as a slave or a child (which is probably what made it 'good' and 'normal' at the same time), it was plainly sick for me to pretend to be the mother of my twenty-seven-year-old boyfriend, the man I wanted to love as a man. I promised myself I would not get into that, because even if it worked, how could it go on? But when we played Mommy it did work, and it did go on. For years, the only way we could ever make love.

I didn't mind, not really, not too much, not at first. The cooing, the sweet petting and comforting *shhh shhhhs*. All of that was fine, as long as it was just me doing the acting. But then, with Mommy, Glen started to get in on the act. The predictable things at first, an obediently whispered *Yes Mommy* or fearful *Does Daddy know?* Then his body started to get into it. His large hands touched my skin as a child's would, tentative and pleading. He would curl his knees up into his chest on the bed until they were soothingly pressed down by my hands. When I was 'teaching him how to kiss,' he even allowed himself to let a string of drool hang down from his mouth across the pillow in boyish wantonness.

'Glen! You don't have to take it *that* far! I'm the one who *cleans* these sheets, you know!'

'Don't be angry, Mommy,' he'd say, flush, and jab his thumb in his mouth.

'Stop it. The game's over.'

'Don't tell Daddy. I'll be good. Don't tell Daddy, Mommy.'

It made me ill, turned me off, sent off moral alarm bells in my head. But it made Glen hard, the only thing that did. And if this was what it was going to take to make us work, I could live with it. Lose a little pride, I told myself. Sex is never dignified, and nobody has to know a thing. But this didn't stop me from wanting to know why Glen wasn't normal, why our lives had to take this desperate turn in order to do what should come naturally. I couldn't ask him about it, of course. Whenever I came close he became secretive, dark-eyed, abrupt. And I knew well enough that to press him could bring another side out of him. The side that cracked the bridge of your glasses off your face and left your front teeth wobbly at the roots.

* * *

Glen sells mutual funds. The company he works for leases a floor in a tower on de Maisonneuve, down near Ogilvy's, the fur stores and $7-a-drink strip clubs. His office is a square space surrounded by orange, spongy portable walls and a desk with a multi-buttoned phone on it. His time is spent calling up clients, shooting the breeze, letting them in on tips. Most of the time they go for it: the men after a discussion of the Canadiens' chances in the playoffs, the housewives and widows once they're through talking about their fussy, talk-show-filled days. They all love him, they channel any spare money his way. It's not trust they feel exactly, they just don't want to disappoint him.

I know because I'm the same way. When he's up and going, Glen's an inflated, happy boy. Big, cute, excited and sexy. You'd do anything rather than let him down. When clients call him at home I hear him say, 'It all depends on the risk you want to take.' The inflection of his voice suggests that high risk is always preferable. Why not? Live a little.

I choose Bond Funds. They're safe, creeping along year after year, making nobody millionaires. Glen calls me 'sweet' for this, but somehow I feel he's let down when I don't go for the flashier options. He knows there are people out there who do.

Sweet is not what I want to be, it's not enough for a man like Glen. It stands for insignificance. There was a time when I would never have been mistaken for sweet, but here I am, sticking weekly grocery budgets up on the fridge door with magnets shaped like fruit and reading women's magazines for the recipes.

What I want to know is what it is inside of me that makes me love without questions. When I think about Glen I always think of that Frank Sinatra song, the one about a man with few regrets who did it his way. Nobody could read him or change his mind or make him entirely happy through actions of their own. Why do I love him for that, for the force of will that keeps everything to himself?

* * *

I know what the X-rays will show before I get them. I'm never surprised when I see the black lumps sitting in the bottom of lungs, clustered in breasts, clinging to intestines. I know not because there's something predictable about the patients – it's not bags under the eyes or brittle fingernails that give them away. I'm just never surprised, that's all. Healthy-looking ones can decline overnight, and paper-skinned corpses can bounce back and be telling jokes and pinching asses within a week. If there's one thing this job has gotten me used to it's the silliness in the selectivity of death, the way it pops out from behind the curtains and makes a face.

One of my professors at school, a wiry-haired Scot, always said that the radiologist is the modern-day seer, someone who looks into the entrails and predicts the future. But he was only partly right. I predict the *ends* of futures. Looking under the skins of people every day has led me to think directly about death. I'm interested in its technique, the way it crouches, sneaks and lunges. I'm not into the spiritual part of it, like those people on *Geraldo* who've had a near-death experience and come back to say it's all right, it's bright and warm and your friends will be there in heaven. It would be nice if it was like that, although I'm pretty sure it's just nothing and darkness.

I'd miss Glen if I died, though. The thought of him in our apartment all on his own makes my chest feel tight and my eyes sting. He'd be lost. Can't even boil an egg. And who would he talk to, sleep with, hold close and call sweet baby? The thought that there could be another after me is worse than Glen going first. Way worse. And it's not the sex part that kills me, either. It's him doing the little, humble, awkward, good things for another. Sitting on the edge of the tub while I have a bath and calling me beautiful while he scrubs my back. Unexpectedly pulling me onto his lap as I walk by his chair and kissing the inner ridges of my ears. Catching him staring at me with a hardened but longing look I want to get inside of but can't.

* * *

On Victoria Day last year Glen and I took a picnic down to the conservation area along the Lachine Canal. We sat by the slightly rotten-smelling water and ate summer sausage and cheddar sandwiches. It was a great day, we even called it that, our mouths full of food. 'What a great day,' both of us say, gazing off toward the concrete grain silos down at the St. Lawrence piers. Then, out of nowhere, sitting in the first real heat of spring, sipping a couple of quart bottles of Export, Glen starts sniffling.

'Allergies?' I say. Then I realize he's weeping. 'What's wrong, baby?'

'I just can't handle it.'

'What?'

'I don't know. This. Being happy. I can't –'

He buries his head in my neck and sobs powerfully, shaking my shoulders and bumping my chin up and down. When he's wiped his face on the bedsheet we're lying on, I ask him what he meant.

'Nothing.'

'C'mon. You were crying.'

'I hate it when you use that mother voice.'

'You seemed to like it this morning.'

'That's different. And don't talk about that like it's a joke.'

'I'm sorry. I won't talk like your mother any more.'

'Not *my* mother, you're not *my* mother. When you talk like that it makes me feel like you're looking down on me. Like you think it's all so fucking funny.'

'I'm not. I don't.'

'Forget it.'

'No. Let's talk.'

I move to put my arms around his neck, fatten my lips for a kiss, but he pushes me away. The tears are entirely gone now. Instead there is a quick, flashing anger, a swelling of the cheeks and nostrils.

'Bitch. Stop treating me like a fucking child,' he says, but his face *does* look like a boy's, tightened by a playground humiliation. And then he really pushes me, slams the back of my head against the trunk of a willow next to us.

We pack up and go home in silence, end the day off in the middle while others in the park stay and play Frisbee, doze on blankets, laugh as they try to stay up on new rollerblades. Walking away, I avoid their eyes as they stop to watch Glen viciously throw empty beer bottles into the canal. Everybody notices that he does it bitterly and with purpose, as though the bottles themselves were responsible for bringing him some particular misfortune or calling up a bad dream.

* * *

Mr. Donoghue went ahead and died last Sunday. All the growing black shapes in his X-rays finally took him over, cut off the blood to some vital organ or blocked an essential passage of air. It happened at night, after visiting hours, without anyone around. They pump them so full of painkillers at that stage the doctors tell the relatives they never feel any discomfort, but I know that's not true. If you've ever actually watched somebody die you know that's not true.

Mr. Donoghue's wife was the only one who visited him. He told me they had two children, but they had both moved out west and had children of their own now and couldn't get away. He said he understood, there was no need to forgive them for anything.

'I just need Ellen,' he'd say, his bony hand clinging to his wife's when I come in to get him ready for another scan. She would smile up at me weakly, her lap full of balled-up Kleenex and mystery novels. I never heard her speak to him, but you could see the love she had for him in her eyes. Well, not exactly love. Loyalty, resignation, a wearied forgiveness.

I look at the Donoghues and try to see Glen and I like that, years down the line. It's not the aging that bothers me. It's getting to that point, right at the end, and still not knowing what the man you've been with the whole time is about, who he is. You might come to the end without even having the first idea.

Lately I've been having this thought: I want to put Glen under an X-ray. But a special kind, one that shows you all the delicate, buried, unscientific things. Something other than grey organs, arteries, and bones. I need to see something more than the unreadable shadowy masses, to decide if they're malignant or benign.

1001 Names and Their Meanings

I'M NOT SAYING it didn't happen. I'd been drinking, it was late, she was crying, wouldn't shut up, I was reaching for her soother and she sort of kick-spun out of my arms. But I didn't drop her. That's what I keep trying to tell the judge, that the whole story's true except for the part that I did it intentionally. I tell him I don't do *anything* intentionally. Babies just get away from you sometimes.

Allie sitting beside her lawyer, tears bleeding their way down her face leaving criss-crosses before splashing onto her good white blouse. Everything in our apartment is furry with dust and nobody's made a trip to the laundry in months but today her blouse is bleached clean. When had she done that? She never seems to sleep – maybe that's when she lives her life, when me and the baby are off in LaLaLand. We're like that a lot, the baby and I.

The judge is steamed, literally damp with bother, beading down on me with his made-up mind. He started out impatient, like this had taken up too much time already after five minutes. *You're the piss-tank who dropped his baby.* That's what he wants to say, but instead I hear, 'Let me say at this preliminary point in the proceedings that this court finds your actions grossly irresponsible, Mr. Stewart.'

Allie tells the judge about the fights. She shows scars. Raises her blouse and points to a burgundy lightning bolt below her breast. That's where she slammed against the fridge door handle. And there, that's a can opener. Cries and cries, but she gets everything across, remembers everything, times and dates. When she's done she looks up at the judge and he tells her she's done well, she can step down now, thank you for what must have been very difficult. She nods and wipes her nose with her hand and tucks in her blouse. I've never seen anything so white.

Cops take the stand, flipping through notebooks. They don't look familiar in any particular sense, but Montreal cops all look the same. Then I remember that cops everywhere look the same. And they know so much. *At 1:40 a.m. proceeded to 1427 St. Denis on a reported domestic disturbance. Arrived to hear shouting from the upstairs apartment. A neighbour, Ms. Perell, held the accused's child in the hallway....* Tell stories of bruises and fractures and empty bottles of Ballantine's built up into a pyramid next to the TV. All of them call me Mr. Stewart, but they didn't call me that on those nights. Then it was asshole. *All right, asshole. Let's go.*

The judge asks me about job prospects, and I tell him I'm looking but it's tough. Never finished my degree. My French isn't so good. We were talking about moving somewhere else, but in what seemed like a total of two days Allie became pregnant, I dropped out of school, and the collection agencies were calling and calling until a guy from Bell with screwdrivers hanging from his belt took the phone away.

The judge wants to know if there isn't any family somewhere to help.

We're both the only child, me and Allie, I say. That's why we got along at first probably. A pair of spoilt brats, I tell him. But the judge doesn't smile.

Parents?

Hers are dead, mine live in Victoria and say their budget is limited. Besides, they say, couldn't you have used a rubber?

I looked for jobs but there was nothing so I painted the baby's room. Allie chose the colour. I called it yellow, and every time she said, No, Jason. It's mustard.

But that's not true, Allie's lawyer says. You found a few jobs, you just couldn't hold them. Not with your drinking.

And I say, Yeah, but I painted the baby's room. With a brush, because the rollers cost six-fifty.

But the lawyer says, I have affidavits from previous employers right here. You were fired because you took days off without calling in, and when you did show up you were late and smelled like a distillery.

And I say, Well, if that's what they say. I guess that's right.

The judge asks me if I understand what a restraining order is.

Of course I know what it is. It means I have to stay away.

That's right. So you can't hurt anyone anymore.

The judge is signing something, a clerk is handing him orange sheets of paper. He says, Do you understand?

But my daughter?

Asks if I love my daughter and I tell him I'm her father.

I know that, but do you *love* her?

I'm her father.

* * *

Toronto is a long street with doorways that cost too much to enter. I stay close to home and drink where I work. It's on the next block, a burger and draft place with a thirty-inch colour screen on top of the fridge. I'm the cook. Never cooked before, even for myself, but now I'm deep frying the shit out of whatever comes my way. Nobody says the food is good, but nobody complains, either. The owner lets me run a tab when I get off at ten and move to the other side of the counter, dirty my thumb on the newsprint in the free weeklies and work my way through half-price doubles until it's time to go home.

You'd be surprised how low your heating bills would be if you lived above a laundromat. That's my place now, a one-bedroom over the Koin-Kleen on Bathurst. Below the mattress and linoleum is the rumbling warmth of the tumble driers. Saves me thirty bucks a month. A good part of that money ends up wasted on postage for letters I've written to Allie but never send. Sometimes I even make it as far as the mailbox before folding the envelope up into a dense square and flicking it into the trash.

So it goes on: move away, close things up, wake up, go to bed. Forget, half forget. Here, not here. A life falling away like the booster rockets on the Space Shuttle. There go my parents, leaving nothing but the smell of Brylcreem and wet woollen sweaters returned too quickly to airless closets. School is a mirage of boredom, too much coffee and an endless chasing and scraping for dope. Home an idea borrowed from television Christmas specials. Love a face you struggle to fix but it's gone, leaving a ghostly absence, like how they say it is with amputees and their lost limbs.

When she was pink-faced and pregnant Allie bought a book
called *1001 Names and Their Meanings* at a used bookstore on
Milton. On the cover was a picture of a baby floating in space
with the sun behind its head like a halo. It's just hanging there
among the stars, big gummy smile, nameless. The book was
one of those '#1 Bestseller!' paperbacks designed for parents
who have no idea what to call their kids once they've rejected
their own parents' names and those of soap opera characters.
Allie worked her way through it as if there was going to be an
exam at the end. Sitting at the kitchen table, her belly rising
over the edge, shouting out names and the story of their symbolic origins. It's full of ones nobody would ever give their kid,
like Fritzi, Halcyone and Esmerelda for girls, Calvert, Everard
and Dagwood for boys.

'How about Brunhilda? Armoured warrior maiden,' Allie
says.

'I like it. I can see her flying around on a broomstick. And if
it's a boy?'

'Then it's gotta be Griswold. From the gray forest.'

I ask about Allie's name.

'Allison. It means: Little truthful one.'

'That's about right. What about me?'

'Let's see. Jason. It says you are the Healer.'

'What's that mean?'

'You can heal, I don't know. That's all it says.'

'Somebody got that wrong,' I say, and Allie turns her head
to me for a split second, and her eyes say *You got that goddamn right*. But it's not hateful, not just now. Sometimes you
can know how bad things really are or how they're going to get
and still feel all right, holding everything off for the moment.
All of our good times were that way. Borrowed, stolen, suspended. Never happy with life itself, with what was really
going on, but one step back from it. Like the last months of
Allie's pregnancy. The sex was especially good then, I remember. Something about the increased blood flow and her need
for extra nourishment. That's what Allie said. In her third
trimester we stayed in bed most mornings, rising only to get
take-out coffee or bring in a plate of toast. Allie laughed that I

could make her come just by looking at her. That's the funny part. Only a few months later we couldn't look at each other at all without something foul starting up between us.

When was it? When did my good-for-a-few-laughs drinking turn to twenty-six ounces a day, my readiness to argue turn to back-handed slaps into bedposts? I could say it happened gradually, but it feels like there was a choice made, a point when I decided to lose my life. But is that right? I didn't *lose my life*. It's more that there wasn't a single moment that I felt it was mine any more. The baby, an apartment with floors that all slanted to the west, whisky starting with *Oprah*, a shoebox on the kitchen table stuffed with demands for immediate payment. Allie waking with a necklace of fingertip bruises, eyes purple and shut. It all just arrived.

During the year after the baby was born Allie gave me a lot of chances. Left numbers of free counselling services on my pillow or, when I was sober, let me make promises never to hit her again. She said if I didn't stop, she would leave. Despite everything I didn't want that. The thing is through all of this I wasn't unhappy. Not exactly. No, I don't think I was unhappy.

But I didn't stop. Spent a week in the can on an assault charge, came home with real tears and five thousand I love yous and still didn't stop. Just moved into anger more and more, made myself at home in it. The apartment became so small it seemed that Allie was always right in front of me, her lips moving and her eyes trying to find mine, and I had to push her out of the way so I could breathe. All through it Allie keeps reaching out to me, offers something, she has to. *There's always something decent in the want ads*. Fuck you. *Can I talk to you for three seconds?* Can you shut up for three seconds? *I want this to work*. What? Want what to work? After a while the fighting stops and is replaced by something close to silence. There aren't arguments, I don't touch her, there isn't anything. No efforts, apologies, promises. Allie sticks the court summons that comes in the mail on the fridge with magnets shaped like strawberries. We both wait for our lives to change.

And the baby cries and cries. Does little else, aside from sleep in two-hour spurts and attach herself to Allie's breasts, which have grown heavy and pale under my second-hand knit sweaters (the only things she wears). Allie tries to get me to change her and give her baths at night, but I make up excuses, lie about having to get something at the store, I need to get some sleep. When she cries at night I play possum until Allie rolls out of bed.

Except once, the night they ask me about in court. I don't want to talk about how she fell. I don't want to talk about it because before that happened, there was this good feeling I had with her. Alone together, just me and her. Allie had a wipe-out head cold so that when the baby started crying I nudged her with my toe but her body felt loose and dead. The baby kept crying like the world was about to end. I went to her room and pulled her up from her crib, walked to the living room and held her by the front window. Outside there was a wind-wild snowstorm, lit Sunkist orange by the streetlights. I whisper unnecessary *shh shhs* because she's already asleep in my arms. The flashing yellow lights of the city snowploughs glance into the room, off the ceiling, reach into the kitchen and lick at the bedroom door.

And in my arms the baby sleeps. A sky-opening blizzard outside but her eyes are sealed shut, her face turned in to my chest. I stand looking down on St. Denis, naked and awake, ten thousand draughts passing through the window cracks. The baby sleeps, each breath a good-smelling squeak. Shivering in bare feet on the cold, slanted floors, the room twice as large at night, watching the streets fill with white silence. I whisper *Is this what you wanted? Did you wake Daddy up to see the snow?* as the baby sleeps in my arms.

* * *

Now I'm the guy who gets postcards. They're all kept laughy-light, fluffed up with stupid details. It's like I'm the crazy grandfather locked away somewhere who can't understand and isn't interested in hearing anything more than that. *Everybody's happy, nothing to worry about, the weather's fine, glad you're not here.*

There's been even fewer of those than usual, in fact nothing for three months, when I get one postmarked in Montreal but with a picture of the Miami skyline on the front: *Hi! It's been a warm spring, although rainy. Found a part-time job, a receptionist at a* TV *station (maybe they'll make me a star!). We went to Florida for a week over Christmas; it was good to get away. Allie.* She doesn't ask how I'm doing. Doesn't explain who 'we' is. The worst thing, though, what set a fire off in my gut, is the way the baby was buried in the words but not named. Alison was pretending she didn't even exist, at least not for me. I could tell by the schoolgirl loops of her handwriting and the way she took up all the space with big gaps between the lines that she was hoping that if the baby weren't mentioned that maybe I'd forget, that I'd be saved some anger or pain. But the thing is I haven't forgotten. And I haven't been saved.

It's time to do something.

What?

Something.

With the postcard folded into my wallet I take the subway down to Union Station and buy a ticket with an open return date. I don't check with work, don't call anyone, I'm not thinking at all. Just climb into a window seat, watch half-tamed brush and small-town Ontario backyards and red brick cottages pass into the clustered walk-ups and warehouses of St. Henri. When the train pulls into the Gare Centrale I mimic the other passengers reaching above for their bags, but remember I haven't brought anything. All I have: a second-hand suede coat, two subway tokens, three twenties and a ten.

I take the metro up to the Laurier station, step up into the flash of late afternoon sun. Two blocks north on St. Denis and there's our apartment, a 4 1/2 above a shoe repair store. The thin glass of the old front window has been replaced with double-glazed, and blinds prevent any view inside. I stand in front of the store looking up, wondering if Allie is inside. Wondering if she will come to the window and look down, invite me up for coffee. She will show me photographs of the baby, funny ones of her splashing in the tub, blowing out birthday candles, dressed as a witch for Halloween. We will laugh together, ask what's new, avoid anything awkward or direct. Part with a brief hug at the door.

But none of this will happen. It would be in violation of the court order for one thing. For another if Allie saw me standing below her window she would be terrified, faced with a ghost in a suede coat and beard. Then, always sooner than you'd think, the cops would arrive. Would they remember me? *Didn't you get enough the first time, pal?* No, maybe I didn't. Not even close. *All right, asshole. Let's go.*

I move off St. Denis and head west into the network of wrought-iron stairs and inconsistent, unlikely coloured brick. The sun slips down to the level of the Plateau's jagged antennas and rooftops, splintering shadows over the narrow streets. I seem to know where I'm going. At the corner, a day-care connected to the rear of a church. I remember it from before, Allie saying this is where the baby will go when she's a little older.

About a dozen kids toddle around the small cement yard, screaming at each other in English and French. Most take turns climbing up the slide, collapsing in laughter when their feet slip out on the buffed steel. One girl sits on her own in a sand box facing the street, head lowered in concentration. This is my daughter. Meredith. Old Welsh, meaning Guardian from the Sea. It suited the way her hands automatically raised when Allie held her when she was first born as though breaking the water's surface, reaching for something warm to grab hold of.

I watch the way her mouth and eyes twist and squint as she digs up sand, talks to herself. Talks! Do they learn that fast? Then I see how her face has become her own, recognizable but transformed, a particular little girl's face. Add a head of blond curls and she looks pretty much exactly like me in an old photograph I have. Me at the beach at Lake Huron. Running back screaming from the tide, pretending the water's foam is boiling acid. Yes, she looks just like me at that age, with a little of Allie around the mouth, the half-pout at the edges. That's blood for you. It leaves marks, imprints itself forever in the creases of the face. It's got to be one of the crueller tricks of nature, of families. How many mothers have had to love children who carry the face of absent fathers?

'What are you building?' I ask her. She doesn't look up at first, finishes a thought with her hands.

'A castle. It's a *sand* castle.'

'Of course.'

'Who are you?'

'Nobody. Just a visitor.'

'Why are you a visitor?'

'Because. I don't live around here.'

'Where'd you come from?'

'I'm not sure.'

'Did you come from over the mountains? My mommy says that's where faraway is.'

'Does she? Yes. That's where I'm from, then. From over the mountains.'

'Oh,' she thinks, patting the walls firm. 'And now you're here?'

The sun skulks behind the rooftops, dusk spills out of the alleyways. From all around there is a collection of neighbourhood sounds that together take the shape of familiar music: the Doppler whoop of an ambulance, an old couple shouting at each other in Portuguese, a pregnant cat mewling by the church gates.

'And now I'm here,' I say, and when I lower my hand she waits only the length of a held breath before she takes it.

Previously Published Works

'Elvis,' *The Pillar*, McGill University (Spring 1991)

'Call Roxanne,' *The New Quarterly*, University of Waterloo
   (Spring 1991)

'Magnificent,' *Quarry*, Quarry Press (Summer 1992)

'Somewhere Real,' *The New Quarterly*, University of
   Waterloo (Winter 1993)

'Three Ways to Start the Story of My Life,' *Blood &
   Aphorisms*, Gutter Press (Fall 1994)

'Camp Sacred Heart,' *The New Quarterly*, University of
   Waterloo (Fall 1994)

'Lane,' *Event*, Douglas College (Spring 1995)

'House of Mirrors,' *The Quarterly*, Gutter Press (Summer
   1995)

'The Drums of Montreal,' *Quarry*, Quarry Press (Fall 1995)

'Daytime Masturbator,' *Blood & Aphorisms*, Gutter Press
   (Fall 1995)

'1001 Names and Their Meanings,' *The New Quarterly*,
   University of Waterloo (Fall 1995)

'Sausage Stew,' *Event*, Douglas College (Summer 1996)

'Dime Bag Girl,' *The New Quarterly*, University of Waterloo
   (Summer 1996)

'Kiss Me,' *Descant* (Fall 1996)

ALEX BECKETT

ANDREW PYPER was born in Stratford, Ontario, in 1968. He holds a BA and an MA in English from McGill University and a law degree from the University of Toronto. His stories have been published in *The New Quarterly, Descant, Event, Quarry,* and *Blood & Aphorisms.* **Kiss Me** is his first book.

Andrew Pyper currently lives in Toronto.